YOU

YOU

ALEXIA MUELLE-RUSHBROOK

First paperback edition 2024

ISBNs:

Paperback: 978-1-7392662-7-1

eBook: 978-1-7392662-8-8

www.alexiamuellerushbrook.co.uk

CONTENT WARNING

This book contains themes readers may find distressing. Although descriptions are not overly graphic, themes include, death, murder, violence, drug sale, bullying, domestic abuse, child abuse – including attempted sexual assault and abduction, depression, sex, and profanity.
If you think you might be triggered by any of the above, please reconsider reading *You*.

BOOKS BY THE AUTHOR:

THE MINORITY RULE

THE MINORITY RULE:
BEYOND THE FENCE

THE MINORITY RULE:
INTO THE FOG

THEY CALL ME ANGEL

YOU

For Emma, David, Charlotte, Iona, and Kerry
Your encouragement means more than you'll ever know

At the bottom of the garden lived many creatures
most of which I knew
But there also lived an elusive soul
simply referred to as 'You'

You has no other name or number
no shape with which to define
I'm not even sure they have a colour
because on You no light dares shine

You might ask how I know that You exists
if no eyes have laid on them?
I suppose I too, would ask that
had I not met You when I was ten

It was a chance encounter
a meeting of some sort
One I hadn't planned on
and certainly can't be bought

But now that I have met You
of them, others I must tell
Or maybe warn, for it depends
if You likes you as well

THE BEGINNING

It didn't occur to me until much later, but I spent an unhealthy amount of my childhood in the tool shed. It was, however, a place of peace and solitude for many years, so I cannot say that I regret my time there—*mostly*.

The shed was an ornate mixture of red brick and flint finished with a slate roof—or would have been if it wasn't covered in vines and brambles. It was a structure of three parts: wood, potting, and junk that was essentially hoarded *just in case*—although no one honestly knew exactly what *case* they were waiting for.

My father was a keen gardener. For hours I would watch him prune flowers, root out weeds, and cultivate crops whilst listening to his explanations of each and every plant. For my seventh birthday, he gave me a silver folding knife, a trowel, fork, and gardener's kneeler. My mother thought them ridiculous gifts for my age, but I treasured them. When Dad's friends or business acquaintances came around I hated it because his tone changed completely. He never turned me away though, and I would still sit and listen, holding onto every second—not yet realising how precious those moments were. Sometimes people questioned whether *the girl should go find her mother*, but my father always replied the same way: *She is the future here. Let her stay.*

What *here* was exactly, I did not know. My father had a way of speaking plainly in riddles. He hid nothing and everything, so the true nature of his business, much like my time in the shed, didn't really dawn on me until years later. It was clever really, because when the police came knocking, any questions aimed at me were answered honestly but gave away nothing. He was still arrested for murder and drug dealing—just not because of my wandering tongue.

Afterwards, Mum refused to move house. Uncle Gary repeatedly visited telling her she should, but if nothing else she was a stubborn woman, so the more Gary tried to convince her to move, the more she decided to stay. While Dad's associates rumbled and adjusted, she played the part of a grieving, loyal wife, but once the business split into two, her weekly visits to prison became monthly, to bi-monthly, to never.

Darren moved in somewhere in between. The exact point of his arrival has always been hazy. Aged seven, I would have said he was one of my father's associates. Aged eight, perhaps he was one of Dad's guards sent to watch over us in his absence. By eight and a half he was a half-drunken, half-dressed slob with a foul mouth and hard fist.

Despite everything, Mum worshipped him. Sometimes I thought that she had forgotten she had a child. I could disappear down the garden for hours, making my way through the overgrown grass, volunteer crops, and wayward flowers until I reached the shed without even a cursory call out of the kitchen window. No one took me to see him, but in Dad's absence, I continued to tend to the plants and even attempted to grow new ones—often unsuccessfully, but always in the hope that Dad would return and appreciate my efforts.

Wishing to retain my privacy, I avoided the potting window and its view of our grey brick house, instead making my home amongst the junk around the corner. There I lived out of sight and largely unchallenged for three years—until You arrived and changed everything.

Maybe You had always been there. Maybe they had peacefully existed in quiet contemplation amongst the creatures of the garden, wandering the orchard and woods that extended beyond our fence if they required a change of scenery. Maybe You would never have shown themselves had they not been pushed by circumstances too great to ignore. Maybe You was—well, who knows?

All I know is my hiding place for one was exposed and You revealed themself when I needed them the most. Whether right or wrong, you can judge for yourself, but this is my story of my friend, and I, for one, am grateful You exists.

It had been a particularly difficult day at school. Honestly, most days were. Children can be the kindest or the cruellest, and the children in my class seemed to prefer the latter. Even before my father was taken from me, I was the weird girl. The girl whose hair never sat right, didn't wear the *in* clothes, like the popular toys, or fancy the right boys. Needing glasses early on was just the cherry on top. The only difference between pre and post my father's incarceration was how far they were willing to go. Occasional verbal taunts were relatively safe, but no one would dare leave a mark on my father's daughter. Afterwards I was nicknamed *the Jailbird*. Jailbirds, apparently, needed a new level of attention.

Walking out the school gate, my shoulders must have dropped as I saw Darren's truck waiting for me.

"Hey, you ungrateful little shit. Don't give me that look." I tried not to look at him at all. "Do you think you're too good to ride home with me? You can bloody walk for all I care." I didn't answer him as I got into the vehicle—I knew better. Darren scoffed. "You will next time."

Five minutes passed with the only sound coming from the engine and the gentle chink of a half-filled whiskey bottle as it rolled left and right in the central reservation.

Darren tutted. "Aren't you going to ask where your mother is?"

Honestly, it hadn't occurred to me. She hadn't come for me, that was all I needed to know. It wasn't exactly an unusual occurrence. Any kind of appointment could have distracted her—hair and nails were probably the most common, but if not drunk at home, she and her friends were always out somewhere. Finding my own way home had become second nature. I suppose the only difference that day was Mum had been detained in a manner that reminded her of the time and my existence simultaneously.

"Where is Mum?" I asked without turning away from the road. I would play his game for the sake of a peaceful drive home, but that was all.

"At the hospital with Joey."

My eyes shot to Darren's face. His sons' health was probably the only thing he wouldn't joke about.

"What's wrong with him?"

"He fell down the stairs."

Instantly, I wanted to ask if he fell or was pushed, but only that morning I had witnessed Joey standing against the baby gate, fiddling with the catch. Darren never closed it properly, so chances were it was an accident—an avoidable one, but still an accident.

My thoughts caused me to daydream a moment too long, and I was jumped back to reality by a clip around the back of the head. "Have you nothing to say?" With my glasses then halfway down my nose, I stared at Darren, trying to work out what response he wanted. "Your fuckin' brother is in hospital and you just stare into space! Are you fuckin' stupid—or just stone selfish?"

I tried to open my mouth but stuttered. I always stuttered when Darren got angry. I couldn't help it. He glared at me as tears rolled down my cheeks.

Rolling his eyes, Darren let out a sigh. "We're going home. I'll get some food, then we'll go see them. The doctor wants to keep Joey for twenty-four hours under observation."

"So, he should be okay?" I wiped my face with the back of my sleeve.

"He'd better be." Darren's words were an unsettling mix of anxious hope and anger. He didn't speak again until he parked in our driveway. "Get changed. We won't be long."

It crossed my mind to ask to stay behind and do my homework, but I knew better. If Mum and Darren had decided to display a united, happy family at the hospital, that was all there was to it. Instead, I just said, "Sure!" and slid from the truck and ran to the garden gate, down the path I'd carved out for myself like sheep across a field, and almost crashed into the old wooden door. Reaching for the metal clasp, I listened to the familiar click and groan as the door opened. Making a beeline for my little camp bed, I threw myself under the sleeping bag and cried my heart out.

If ten-year-old children have clear intentions, mine was to release the day's stress for a moment, feed the birds, then be changed way before Darren came looking for me. But the day had been long, the torment from the girls in my class exhausting, and the notion that my two-year-old half-brother might be seriously injured weighed heavily on me. In short, I had fallen asleep.

"What the fuck?" Darren's default response to any and everything. "Get up!" He briskly grabbed my arm and pulled me into the sitting position.

His eyes were so dilated, the blue just seemed black—black holes of hatred. Having watched them on TV, it had occurred to me more than once that Darren was like a lion claiming a new pride. He had quickly taken control of the largest portion of my father's business—despite my Uncle Gary's claims to the contrary—and had impregnated his wife within months. The only thing left to do was clear the territory of offspring from the wrong gene pool. Me.

Panicking, I muttered sorry over and over. The stench of alcohol hit me and any hopes of dinner or reasoning with him left me.

Darren's eyes darted around the shed—my home—and he sneered. "I told your mother it was ridiculous leaving you out here. It's not right. It's not normal. I'm going to knock this place down. You'll thank me one day. Or not. I don't really care. You belong locked up like your pathetic old man. I'm not having a fuckin' kid like this under my roof."

"If you leave the shed, I won't be under your fuckin' roof." The words came out of me from nowhere. Only seconds earlier I was preparing to beg him for clemency, but hearing Darren's words cut my tongue, forming a sharpness that I had never dared pronounce before.

Anger and adrenaline tensed every inch of Darren's body. His fist clenched before he grabbed a broom, immediately swinging it across my back. I cowered in pain and fear as he swung again and again. Suddenly the air around me twitched—like the breeze had brought a swarm of flies—and Darren called out. His voice, filled with surprise, turned to a cry as pain and fear struck him. Opening my eyes, I saw him exchange the broom for a shovel. He swung with all the strength that he could muster, but before he hit his target, the twitching air rushed into Darren, thrusting him backwards.

Dust sprinkled from the roof as Darren impacted the wall and a groan slipped out of his mouth as he slowly slid to the floor. His wide eyes held mine, but no recognition registered as his body slumped into a heap. I stared, too afraid to move, and suddenly everything went black.

When I woke up, I was in a hospital bed with a monitor quietly flickering with each heartbeat. My mother was in the chair next to me with my brother curled in her arms. She was asleep but she had clearly been crying because her mascara was everywhere except on her eyelashes. My first thought was *I hope Darren doesn't see her like that.* On numerous occasions he had made it plain that he didn't like emotion or untidiness in his women.

A nurse walked in. "Oh, sweetie, how lovely to see you awake. How are you feeling?"

Before I could answer, my mother woke up. "Finally!" she exclaimed, but with no real warmth or concern for my wellbeing. Mum turned to the nurse. "Where are the police?"

"That can wait for a moment. I'd just like to check—"

"No it can't! We need answers now!"

"Answers to what?" I whispered.

"Who attacked you!"

Darren's face flashed into my mind. The shovel swinging for a victim.

"You remember—right? You remember that you and Darren were attacked?"

Mum's face was earnest. That was plain to see, but I couldn't tell if it was an act like on parents evening or genuine.

My mouth wobbled open and shut as I tried to answer. Both Mum and the nurse waited. "Da—Darren—"

"Yes?" Mum spoke softly but impatience was written in the lines across her forehead.

"Darren attacked me."

Anger flashed across my mother's face. Then pain. Then back to anger as tears spilled down her face. "How can you speak of him so?" Her eyes darted from me to the nurse and back again.

The nurse grimaced sympathetically.

"Mum, I—"

"He died saving you, you know?" A weird choking sound came from her mouth as Mum stifled a wave of emotion.

"Died?" Mum ignored me, so I looked to the nurse. "*Darren died*?" She nodded her head sadly.

Mum's proceeding wails produced a young, female police officer followed by an older man. Between the two of them, they explained that Darren and I were found in a bloody and bruised heap in my shed. All fingerprints on the tools used as weapons were wiped. They didn't tell me then, but I read about it later in a newspaper article—one that was clearly not intended for the more sensitive eyes of the ten-year-old victim. Prints were missing, blood stains were not. Darren split his head open on a garden rake, had slashes all over his arms and legs, and a pair of shearers impaled into his chest for good measure. I was hit with a broom and a shovel. The purple imprints on my body provided evidence where memory did not.

None of it made sense.

No one was ever convicted. The case was cold. Darren had enemies, or so the newspaper said. A continuation of my father's legacy. He got what he deserved.

I don't disagree with the last bit. He did deserve it. But I know it was no burglar and neither was it payback from business.

As I stared into the eyes of the police officer, the memory of air moving, dancing in a focused, angry formation came to me.

My eyes welled and flowed. My skin shuddered with goosebumps. My heart rejoiced and gave thanks.

Finally, I had a friend.

———

Once discharged from hospital, Uncle Gary drove me home. Mum was a mess and barely functioned for weeks. Besides instructing me to *tell the truth and honour Darren's memory when speaking to the police,* Mum had no words for me. Certainly, no words of comfort or remorse. She convinced herself that the burglar story was true, yet in her eyes I could see she blamed me. She was a walking oxymoron.

Joey was passed around Mum's friends until after the funeral, but only Gary truly remembered me. He wanted me to see a therapist. I can't say that the idea appealed to me. I would have been too afraid of saying the wrong thing and incurring Mum's wrath, but the hollow I felt inside when I heard Mum's reply could easily have taken hours for any psychologist to unpack. "What for? She was unconscious. *She* has nothing to be traumatised about."

As soon as I could, I crept down the path to the shed. The police had trampled the garden, ruining my meagre attempts at preserving some of Dad's favourite plants. The shed had been turned inside and out—including the log store which I saw little point in but was less distraught about.

"Hello? Can I come in?" I said, closing the door quietly behind me. Until that day, it had never occurred to me to ask permission to enter what I considered to be mine, yet now the air felt different. Stronger. Inhabited.

On countless occasions I had imagined the presence of a friend living there, yet even in my childish state I put this down to desire rather than fact. Squirrels, birds, mice, and hedgehogs who frequently visited me were the closest to friends that I had. The neighbour's cat was the nemesis of the birdfeeder, so I tried not to encourage his visits by petting him—unless we were in the neutral grounds of the woods. I always knew when he was around because the wildlife disappeared. No one was around now, but I instinctively knew their absence had nothing to do with the cat.

"Thank you." I said, glancing around the room, taking note of what I thought was missing. "You saved me. I know you did. So thank you."

I felt movement around me—as though a being had entered the room and sat beside me. Something told me that I should be afraid, yet I felt alive.

"I'm Cassie." I sighed. "I guess you know that. What shall I call you?" A sound, like rustling leaves, echoed in my ear. *You.* That was all they said. It was all I needed. A name was a name, no matter how unusual or brief.

For months after Darren's death, life continued with little outward change, but internally I felt different. At school I was still tormented. The police continued to believe I was the victim of a burglary, teachers looked at me with pity as my bruises gradually faded, but it didn't stop the taunts. *Jailbird's coming. Quick, be careful, she will bury all our fathers* was a regular chant as I approached. Each day I ate my lunch alone and cried in the toilets, counting the minutes until I could tell You about my troubles. They listened unreservedly. On good days we would skip the fence and watch the wildlife that lived amongst the trees. On wet days we would sit in silence as I did my homework.

Joey recovered from his ordeal, but my mother never really did. She idolised Joey more than ever, pandering to his every whim, and doting on his every move. No such affection was bestowed upon me. Every time I returned from the shed, she scowled. She could not understand how I could bear to walk in there. She moaned to her friends that I must be either heartless or crazy to enter into a place that witnessed so much pain. It didn't occur to her that the house had more distinct memories of brutality. Certainly just as many fists had flown there.

Without Darren to stir up division, Uncle Gary reunited Dad's business. Mum didn't tell me that directly, but I heard her swearing about it to Trisha, Darren's sister. Truthfully, I think she was trying to keep in everyone's good books until she knew which side of her bread was better buttered, but as no one on my father's side took her infidelity kindly, perhaps it was wise that she clung on where she could.

One Friday, Mum had forgotten to collect me again—much to the amusement of Kimberley Jenkins and her heinous friends. They threw pebbles at me until they ran out of worthy ammo and moved to larger stones. I tried my best to ignore them, but one hit me in the back of the head and anger flashed in front of my eyes. The anger should have been directed at them yet I found that my subconscious channelled it towards my mother. If, just for once, she had picked me up on time, I would not have been subjected to Kimberley's idea of fun. My mind raced, I screamed, and ran home with the sound of their jeers in my ears.

Intending to head straight to the shed, I paused on the driveway when I found my uncle unloading boxes into the garage.

"Oh, hey, Cassie," he said, turning around.

"Hey," I replied, peering into the back of the van. "What's going on?"

Gary chuckled. "Just a little rearranging. Nothing to worry about. How's school?" I twisted my mouth. "That good, huh?"

"Yeah." My hand instinctively went to the back of my head where I could feel a patch of dried blood and tears began to well. Normally no one asked, so I could mask my pain easily, yet his simple question sent me over the edge of my self-control.

Unsure how to respond, Gary awkwardly rubbed his chin. Just as he looked like he might answer, Mum burst out of the front door, yelling.

"What are you doing?"

"Good to see you too, Michelle."

Mum grunted. "What's that? I don't want your shit here. Keep it at yours."

"No one puts all their eggs in one basket—not even you," Gary said, nodding at Joey who was tucked under Mum's arm.

"Fuck you, Gary."

"What a charming example you are to your children." Gary seemed sad for a moment. "Have you reconsidered my—"

Mum stormed towards Gary. "*Shut up, now.*" She shot a look at me. "Go away, Cassie. Here, take your brother."

Joey was unceremoniously thrust into my arms. I didn't know what to do with him, but as I definitely wanted to get out of sight, I took him to the kitchen. The door and windows were closed, but the escalating shouting drifted through to us and Joey started to cry. It was a shame that Joey inherited his father's cold blue eyes. Mum's heart may have been frozen to me, but she had beautiful green eyes. Had Joey inherited those,

I probably wouldn't have struggled with him half as much, yet even the slightest glance reminded me of Darren and his ever looming, swinging frame.

Increased screaming outside made Joey howl. The opposite of me, whatever Joey wanted, he got, but that day we wanted the same thing. Silence. So I wrapped him in a coat and led him down the garden to meet the many creatures and hoped that You wouldn't mind.

Opening the door, I apologised to You for the addition and my brother quizzically stared at me. When I didn't explain myself, he turned his attention to the contents of the shed. Most of the tools had gone—either removed as evidence by the police or thrown away by my mother once they were returned—but plenty of junk remained to entertain Joey with.

It felt like You was observing, waiting to pass judgement on the newcomer. I guess I was too. This was my space. The last thing I wanted was to make this a regular playground for my little brother, even though I enjoyed his infantile praise as he perused my sketchbook.

Joey began to play with some half-filled flowerpots that failed to sprout in the spring. Grimacing at the increasing mess, I distracted him by pulling open an old set of draws and handing him six colouring pencils and a fresh pad of paper. Glancing between the used sketch pad and the new one, Joey weighed up his options, but I was a moment too slow understanding his dilemma. With lightning speed, he grabbed my pad and proceeded to decimate my latest garden sketch. It was like he knew I was the proudest of that one and wanted to add his mark. I felt sick.

"Cassie!" My mum's shrill voice called from the backdoor. "Cassie! Get here now!" The house backdoor slammed and the voice approached.

"Where is she?" To my surprise, my uncle was coming too.

Wanting to keep them out of my shed, I jumped up, swung open the door, and ran down the path.

"Yes? Can I help?" I asked, trying not to make eye contact with my mother for any longer than absolutely necessary.

"Your uncle wants you to spend time with him." I looked up at the wrong moment and witnessed a sneer that said *I don't know why*.

The air twitched around me. It felt hot and the memory of Darren's attack came to me, causing panic to race under my skin like an electric current.

"Would that be okay?" Gary said. "I'd love you to—"

A high-pitched squeal from the shed cut Gary off. Instantly, the colour drained from my mother's face, but no one spoke as we ran to the open doorway.

"Joey!" exclaimed my mother, pushing me out of the way. "What is it my baby?"

Still where I left him, Joey was motionlessly sitting on the floor beside my camp bed with the notepad and a black pencil in his hands. His stone-blue eyes stared into the log pile, even after my mother picked him up.

"What happened?" Mum's lips trembled. "What is it?"

"Maybe he saw the neighbour's cat?" It was the first thing I could think of. "He has always been fascinated by it."

Mum peered around the wood pile. "Does it come in here?"

"Sometimes, yes."

"Huh." Mum shuddered. "This place is hideous. Why would you bring your brother here? I'm going to have it knocked down."

A cold chill hit me. Why did everyone want to destroy my home—our home? Instantly I knew that You had heard my mother's words. They were angry.

As if sensing my anxiety, Uncle Gary ushered my mother out of the door. "Let's get a takeaway and talk about this inside."

I didn't understand. One minute they were screaming bloody-murder at each other, the next we were set to eat together. As we silently walked away, Mum took the pad from Joey's hand and tossed it onto the floor.

Stooping to pick it up, I paused when I saw the frantic scribble my brother had produced. There, over my serene garden picture stood a shadow—a mass of dark swirls without end.

MOVING HOUSE

Equally conscious of You's regard for privacy and my mother's desire to knock down the shed, I made an effort to keep everyone separate. I tried to pre-empt her calling me by being in my bedroom early each night. It pained me to reduce my time of peace, but I told myself it was better than seeing the shed destroyed.

Every time Joey drew pictures, I felt a little anxious. The fridge was covered in his doodles, but Mum seemed reluctant to pin up his newfound love of dark swirls. Thankfully, she didn't seem to link this artistic movement with that day in the shed, but I knew who my little brother was attempting to give shape to.

Uncle Gary told me he wanted me to live with him but my mother was refusing. He didn't say it, but the reason for her refusal was obvious. Child support. Dad had ensured I was well catered for—university included; such was the length of his prison sentence—and although my Mum received a healthy sum during their divorce settlement, siphoning money from my support funds was easy pickings.

I was curious about what life with Gary could look like. A permanent move seemed too fantastical, but I wondered if the prospect of moving wouldn't be so bad if I could persuade You to come with me.

Sitting crossed legged on my camp bed, I decided to broach the subject. I was nervous because You had so far refused to go to school with me. Sometimes I thought they might change their mind, but my confidence—my hope—that they might back me up had thus far waned. My new hope was that visiting Gary's might be a compromise—or a stepping stone because the hatred I then felt towards Kimberley and her friends had reached a new level.

Leaving pins in my classroom chair, stones in my coat pocket, and crude notes in my locker had become standard. I neither sat down nor opened anything without extreme caution, but that day they had taken to flicking gum at me. A dozen or more pieces had hit me when a ball became perilously close to lodging into my hair. My long, curly brown locks were hard to tame on a good day. Sticky balls of half chewed pink crap would be impossible without scissors. The girls knew it and giggled with demonic glee as I struggled to free myself.

Running away, I silently cried for help—or to disappear into an invisible realm with You.

Why Kimberley and her friends couldn't leave me alone, I did not understand. The older, more developed I became, the more they seemed to target me. The idea of needing a bra filled me with dread—I knew what would happen to the elasticated straps.

Finishing my account of the day, feeling a confusing mixture of embarrassment, disgust, anger, and depression, I took a deep breath, and said: "If you don't want to help me at school, would you come with me to my uncle's? He has a large shed—I asked him." I paused, waiting for a sign. "Please, I need change—but I also need you."

The air around me shimmered.

My eyes pricked with tears as the room briefly turned black.

You had said yes. I was sure of it.

———

I went to school the next day with a spring in my step. Uncle Gary was picking me up that night and taking me to his for the weekend. He had no family, so I had no one to impress but him. I would make sure I was the niece he wanted to love and keep—not return to my mother whose heart was as grey and cold as our house.

"What are you smiling about?" jeered Kimberly as I walked into the classroom.

I checked the front of the room and sighed. Why was Miss Keets always late?

"I'm talking to you." My eyes returned to Kimberley but my mouth remained closed. This was an exciting day. I would not let her ruin it.

"Did she just sneer at you, Kim?" I glared at Lola. "Ooh, she did! Look at that!"

The room chuckled and frustration rose in me like an overfilled pot of boiling water. "Oh fuck off, Lola," I said, walking to my seat.

Stooping, I rubbed my hand over the dark-grey plastic chair for pins, but before I could complete my check a pair of hands gripped my arms and spun me around.

"What did you just say?" Kimberley's face was inches from mine. Her nostrils flared and my heart raced. A sound—like a rustle of shifting autumnal leaves—rang in my ears. My skin bristled seconds before I felt a hand on the back of my head. It paused, like it was giving me a warning, then suddenly increased the pressure and jolted my head forwards, crashing into Kimberley's.

My eyes boggled, but not from pain—although I will not pretend it didn't hurt—but from untold joy. It might be reasonable to think that being controlled by You would have been distressing. Perhaps it should have been. Perhaps I should have felt guilty seeing blood trickle out of Kimberley Jenkins nose, but I didn't.

I was triumphant.

A stunned silence came over the room. Thirty pairs of eyes bore down on me as I readjusted my glasses, theatrically straightened my jumper and skirt, and sat at my desk. It was only when I looked forward that I realised Miss Keets was also watching.

No one thought to ask why I had headbutted a fellow student. Honestly, I think they all knew why, but my mother was too furious to focus on insignificant details such as me being bullied. To her, the indignity of being questioned by the headteacher was a humiliation too far for further thought.

"You can't go to Gary's now." Mum sighed, navigating the car out of the school gate. "You know that, right?"

"What? Why?" My insides felt like they were collapsing.

"What kind of mother would I look like if your teachers found out that I rewarded you with a weekend away after that little manoeuvre?"

My mind raced, hoping to land on an acceptable argument.

"Shit." Mum hit the steering wheel. "There goes my romantic weekend."

This was news to me.

"Are you seeing someone?"

Mum chuckled.

My heart sank at the thought of her having another boyfriend, but I had to use this information to my advantage. "If you have plans, you could always punish me later. I—"

Mum scoffed. "Don't you worry about that! It's time you grew up and learnt to play properly with your peers. Your father might have encouraged your loner ways, but Darren was right, being the weird kid is just going to make you into a pathetic adult."

The mention of Darren's name turned my stomach. Mum's words cut my soul.

"And the first change is getting rid of that fuckin' shed."

"No, Mum, please, I—"

"Don't waste your breath. I've already called Gary. His guys are coming round next week to pull it down."

"No! You will—"

"Enough, Cassie, enough. I can and will."

Mum parked the car outside the hairdressers and semi dragged me into the salon. I was positioned in the window seat with my homework and told to consider the error of my ways. Had I been inclined to do so it would have been difficult to concentrate on anything. All I could hear was my mother recounting her disappointment while Dee, the hairdresser, empathetically tutted in all the right places. Together they reduced me to *she* and *her* and *it*, unanimously condemning me without an ounce of restraint as though I were not in the room.

I yearned to know if You had heard.

Silently crying, I wondered if You, my only friend, would leave me when their home was gone?

My weekend task was to remove anything I considered valuable out of the shed. With so few possessions, it did not take long. Joey sat on the grass watching me but he would not enter the shed. To my knowledge, he never went in there again and seemed anxious as I sprang in and out like an agitated shrew. Every time I spied one of my creature friends, I burst into tears, apologising that they would soon need to find a new spot to visit.

The cruelty. The totally unnecessary cruelty was unfathomable to me.

Gary turned up on Saturday afternoon with a flatpack shed.

"Where's that going?" I asked cautiously.

"There." Mum pointed to a small spot a few meters from the backdoor. "I'm fed up with wandering down the garden in my pyjamas for wood. The woodstore is coming up here and the rest is going in a skip." There wasn't a hint of sorrow in her tone.

Too upset to speak to anyone, I spent the weekend in the shed, taking in the shape of each brick as though I could somehow preserve it with memory alone. You felt distant, and I think that was the hardest thing of all. They were there, but not. Perhaps they too were packing their otherworldly things.

I left You a note pinned to the door:

You can always come and live in my bedroom. I know it's not the same. But what's mine is yours, for there's no need to limit yourself again. Although you prefer the bottom of the garden, in truth your home could be with me. If this doesn't work, let's run away. Yours always, Cassie.

The next morning the note was nestled in my left slipper by my bed. As my eyes cracked open and focused, I panicked, fearing that my mother had seen it.

I was sure to get a beating if she had.

Spinning myself into the sitting position, I caught sight of an object in my right slipper. Kneeling beside my bed, I cautiously lifted the pink fluffy slipper and upended the contents into my hand. Joey was not really old enough to play such pranks, so my mind quickly dismissed his potential involvement, but I had not yet ruled out some kind of cruel act of my mother's.

A red scented candle and plastic lighter dropped into my hand.

I didn't understand. Was my mother telling me that I smelt? Possibly.

Mum shouted up the stairs. "Cassie! Get up! School! Now!"

"Coming!" I knew better than to not answer.

Laying the candle and lighter on my desk, I reached for my left slipper and picked out my note. My eyes were instantly drawn to a waxy mark under the words *yours always*.

With a renewed spring in my step, I quickly dressed and ran downstairs, ready to tackle a new day.

———

The day took some tackling. My class was on red alert and Kimberley was the alarm bell. Miss Keets pulled us both from the room to *have a little word*—which involved us apologising to one another. There was a shift in Kimberley's eye. Part hatred, part fear. I had become something else to her. No longer was I just a weak target, I was an adversary to take down.

A knot in the pit of my stomach twisted. Even I knew headbutting my way out of school would solve nothing—and You, despite the morning's note, seemed woefully absent, perhaps feeling guilty for getting me into trouble in the first place. I couldn't bring myself to regret my actions. All I could regret was future war.

Yet war was coming. Kimberley's expression told me so. Her best friend, Lola, tripping me as I walked past just confirmed it.

"Maybe you need new glasses?" Lola innocently said, tapping me on the back. "I'd hate to see you fall."

Miss Keets nodded approvingly. I wanted to swear at her for her naivety, but instead sat down. Distracted, I forgot to check my chair and immediately paid for it as the point of two pins dug into my legs.

Sniggers rippled around the room but I refused to openly acknowledge the pain I was experiencing. For two hours I sat without moving any more than absolutely necessary. When the bell finally rang, I waited for people to start moving before slowly peeling myself off the chair and allowing a small gasp to leave my lips.

Instantly, ecstatic giggles erupted from Kimberley and Lola who stood in the doorway.

I felt my insides boiling.

"Ignore them," a voice behind me said.

My head whipped around to see Nic leaning on his desk. My heart skipped. It always skipped when I saw him. Heck, I think everyone's heart skipped when they saw him. On the day they were giving out looks, Nic was at the front of the queue with a hall pass, extra lunch money, and a college scholarship all at once. Thankfully, he was also one of the nicest kids in my class.

"Easier said than done, but I know." That sentence was probably five words more than I had said to Nic all term, but he still had a way of disarming me. It was a pity he didn't exercise that effect on his friends instead of quietly observing.

Nic nodded, picked up his bag, and walked towards the exit. Suddenly he stopped, ruffled his hair, and said, "Er, you may want to check your back," then walked away.

I had to take my jumper off to reach it, but that bitch had stuck a sanitary towel to my back. In red ink was written *Jailbird's new wings.*

———

Standing on the edge of the driveway, I could not believe what I was seeing. Two fire engines had screamed into position, wasting no time in blasting water at our house as the local residents watched.

Apparently oblivious to my presence, an old lady muttered to her friend. "It's not that surprising. That family has more enemies than hot dinners."

"Do you think this was deliberate?" her friend replied, putting her hand over her mouth.

"Of course. That, or the wife wanted an insurance pay out after her partner's suspicious demise and her filthy husband got locked up. Someone has to pay for her."

"True." The second woman tutted. "Good riddance."

"Good riddance."

Anger raged in me. "Excuse me," I said politely. Shock and embarrassment struck the women's faces as they gazed at me. "We are standing right here. Have you no decency?"

One lady stared with her mouth flapping.

The other recollected herself and sneered. "Huh. Apple didn't fall far, did it?"

I wanted to point out that my mother would have sworn and my father would have threatened to shoot her, but I shook my head, turned on my heels, and answered my own question: "I guess you don't."

At that moment, my mother arrived. She hardly had time to pull on the handbrake before she got out of the car, screaming. A firefighter held her back as she cried out my name. It was probably the only time she showed me any kind of concern. Weirdly, I wish I had been recording it, but as the firefighter pointed in my direction, I stepped forward and relieved her of her distress.

"What happened?" she demanded of the firefighter.

It took hours to get a clear answer, but when the answer came back, I knew it was You.

"A candle, Mrs Reilly. One was left burning in your bedroom."

"Good riddance to ghosts," Mum said as we drove away from the remains of my childhood home. In some ways, I shared her sentiment, but I couldn't help smiling at the red brick and flint shed as it stood victoriously at the bottom of the garden. All of us moving into Uncle Gary's would present its challenges, but bizarrely I felt that a change might do us good.

You hadn't visited me since the fire, but as the house disappeared out of sight, I knew in my heart that they would find me. It was impossible to entertain even a glimmer of an opposing thought.

A NEW SHED

Gary's house was on the other side of town. The driveway was gated and the house so newly built that pigeons hadn't had time to poop on it yet—that, and Gary had covered the roof in spikes to keep them away. Our old house was set back from the road and wasn't small but each room at Gary's had space in abundance. Almost too much. Ornaments and art pieces were strategically positioned inside and out, marking a corner, or providing something to circle, but also making the place scream bachelor pad, not family home.

While Gary gave us a tour of the interior, my eyes continuously wandered through the bounty of glass in search of a spot that I might now call home. Joey ran along the hallway, slapping his hands gleefully onto the glass each time he paused. I saw my uncle grimace and felt sorry for him, however, I cannot say his face looked regretful.

Perhaps he too, yearned for laughter to fill his heart. Unfortunately, I just wasn't sure that our family had enough heart left to fill. That was Dad. He was the glue and without him, nothing seemed to stick.

As soon as my mother took Joey to bed, I stepped into the garden. The light was fading, but I could see the silhouette of a large greenhouse on the right-hand side of the garden. Gary had previously assured me that he had a shed, and I could only hope that the greenhouse was not what he meant. I couldn't see You nor I inhabiting a greenhouse all year round although I liked the idea of tending crops again—if my uncle would let me.

Knowing You's preference for secluded spots, I continued to survey the garden. A pang of disappointment struck me when I couldn't find a shed, yet the dusky light provided some hope in the form of a little patch of trees at the back of the garden—not truly a wood, more of a copse, but I felt sure there would be creatures for You and me to befriend there.

A sadness hit me as I thought of the creatures I left behind. Seeking solace, I wondered if You would bring them too.

"Penny for them?" Uncle Gary casually wandered across the grass towards me.

"Something like that." I sighed, hoping my response was appropriate. I had heard that expression numerous times, but being on the cusp of my teenage years, I didn't honestly understand it. I did, however, always want to present myself as mature to adults—even if I felt the opposite. I needed someone to accept me because it was as sure as hell that children didn't.

After a moment's silence, Gary said, "So, you like sheds?"

When put like that, I felt decidedly unadult-like, but I answered anyway.

"Yeah. You said you had one?"

"That one is a bit snug," he said, pointing to a small, wooden shed tucked on the far side of the greenhouse. "It's full of bits and bobs, so I wouldn't use that one. "That, there—" Gary paused until he was satisfied I was focused in the right direction. "That would make a lovely teenage hideout, don't you think?"

Around the corner of the house, tucked behind the oversized garage, stood a building—like a studio apartment, I suppose. Speechless, I followed Gary as he walked up to the front door, pulled a key from his pocket, and let himself in. After turning on the light, he gestured for me to enter. A reverence came over me. It was as though I had been granted entrance into a chapel during a time of prayer. There was a peace, a silence, that I really didn't want to disturb, and yet I desperately wanted to look around.

Immediately, I felt welcomed. It was as though someone had taken all of the warmth that should have been in the house and blown it into this little structure. I say little, but the apartment boasted a kitchenette, bathroom, office studio area-cum-living room, and bedroom.

"I thought you could maybe make this yours?" Gary said a little shyly. "It needs someone to show it some life, and I think you might be the one to give it."

"Really?" My skin felt like it was beaming.

"Of course. It's yours."

"No it ain't." My mother appeared in the doorway. "Gary, don't go giving her ideas of grandeur."

"Michelle, I told you, she can—"

"No, Gary, just no." Mum walked into the room, scanning each item and wall. "I told you. This is a temporary move until I get sorted."

"It doesn't have to be. I—"

"It does." Mum flapped her arms. "Look, I'm grateful. Truly grateful. But you're acting on wishes which aren't fair to anyone, least of all—"

"I want Cassie to have this place. It is hers."

"No, it isn't. A few weeks, tops, then we'll be outta here."

Even I couldn't believe how quickly she was ruining this for me. "Mum! Please, can't we—"

"Gordon and I are moving in together. We had planned it before. We just need to find a place, that's all. The bloody fire just expedited things."

"Who is Gordon?" I'd never heard his name before. Gauging by Gary's face, neither had he.

Mum had previously hinted at having a new boyfriend, and I had vowed to myself that I would be ready for whenever it happened—but I wasn't.

My skin pricked with fear.

"Can't I stay here and you—"

"Absolutely not. I am your mother, and you *will* stay with me."

Staring into my mother's eyes, I felt the weight of her decision but no overwhelming wave of affection. I was sure that she viewed me akin to a family heirloom—an antique, like something you'd keep in the attic and begrudgingly drag from house move to house move in the hope that one day it'll increase in value. Something told me that value was in the form of a pay cheque now and nursemaid when she was old.

For the record, I had no intention of wiping her arse.

Arguing was pointless.

That night, I slept in my new shed—my studio—and dreamt of a life there. But as I woke, cruel reality washed over me as I recalled the brevity of this reprieve. It wasn't fair. My mother ruined everything.

The tree outside my window suddenly rustled.

A branch scratched the glass pane.

Jumping out of bed, I opened the window and called to my friend.

You, at least, had heard me.

I tried to savour the time I had at Gary's but it was too short lived. Most days when I came home from school, two or more of Gary's friends were leaving—sometimes even if he wasn't home. I envied the number of people he was friends with. He made it look easy. The only friends I could make were with woodland creatures, plants—who were technically a captive audience—and an unknown being with no form.

Mum disapproved of my interest in Gary's horticultural efforts, but one evening when she was out, Gary showed me around his enormous greenhouse. It irritated me to think it, but I immediately thought how much Dad would have loved it. Memories of him had become extra painful as fear of never seeing him again had mixed with resentment for him getting arrested and leaving me at my mother's mercy.

Oddly, I was less concerned about the murder.

While I was mid-thought, Gary asked me how school was going. He caught me off guard and my eyes began to well as the day replayed in my mind. Kimberley Jenkins had waited for me after school with three of her friends. Between them they had laid a rope across the path ahead of me. I should have seen it, but I was staring at the watercolour I had completed in art class and marvelling at the merit badge I had been awarded by the teacher for my efforts. Just as I stepped around the corner, the rope went up, cutting into my ankles, sending me and the painting into a huge puddle.

The girls roared with laughter while I wrung my picture out in despair.

"Why?" I cried.

Kimberley laughed. "Why? Because you're an arrogant little shit who needs to learn some manners!"

Suddenly, Lola skipped up behind me, snatched my picture and handed it to Kimberley. "I don't see what the fuss is about. My cat could do better." Kimberley turned the picture to her friends and they dutifully laughed.

The picture was ruined, but I wanted it back. It could still go in my diary as the painting *that was*. A group of boys arrived and instantly saw what was happening. They looked at me pitifully but jeered with their friends when I went to retrieve my work.

Kimberley pushed me backwards, slamming me into the wet for a second time, then proceeded to tear the corner of the page. In hindsight, I should have walked away at that point because my obvious distress fuelled her cruelty. Jubilant, she ate the torn piece. Anger raged through me and my body tensed, ready to tackle that bitch to the ground when a calm enveloped me. The air twitched and suddenly I knew that all I needed to do was watch.

You grabbed Kimberley's tongue and twisted it until she screamed. She must have bitten herself as a small drip of blood dribbled down her chin seconds before You pushed her backwards, causing her to stumble to the floor. As she panted with blurred, petrified vision, a strange hush froze the group.

No one dared move—except me.

The glimmering particles of my friend would not harm me. Reaching for my painting, I theatrically took it from her hand, and tutted as I walked away. Seeing Nic's freaked out eyes, I briefly felt a pang of remorse, but then I reminded myself that he was the same as the rest of them. All of them had stood by as I was tormented, so why should I feel bad when the roles were reversed?

When my uncle asked what was wrong, I went to my bag and pulled out my ruined painting.

"It fell in a puddle," I explained.

"Oh, what a shame," my uncle replied. "Can you paint another?"

A chuckle slipped out. "No, but I can."

———

Not only did Gordon not have a shed, but he didn't even have a garden. He rented a two-bedroom flat on the third floor of an estate that some of Dad's associates controlled but would never actually want to live on. I only knew the latter part because I heard Gary and Mum shouting in the kitchen the day before we moved. I loved that Gary was trying, but I knew in my heart it was no good.

Whatever I thought about Darren, he was at least relatively good looking for an adult—evil, but not ugly. What Gordon lacked in beauty, he made up for in muscle. Each morning, I was subjected to viewing them as he strutted around the apartment in his white vest and jogging bottoms.

Mum couldn't keep her hands off him. She was firmly in the lovestruck puppy phase, and I began to doubt whether she would notice if I slipped off to Gary's and never came back. To my surprise, even Joey began to be forgotten, and I found myself not only sharing a room with him but tending to his needs—both physical and mental—more and more.

With trepidation, I recognised that animalistic glare in Gordon's eyes as he viewed Joey. He was the son from the last man, the bloodline that had no place in his heart nor his territory. It made me afraid—and angry. It also kept me rooted, for even though the temptation to run away and not look back was strong, I knew that I couldn't run with my little brother in tow.

But I badly wanted to run.

Although I said that Gordon viewed Joey with a bloodlust—that was true—he seemed to lust in a different way when he saw me. Always ahead of my class, if dressed right, I could easily pass for older than I was. Overnight my chest had sprung, my legs shot out, and my hips widened. At school I was jeered for it. At home I was petrified of it.

Each night, I slept in my brothers' bed. I told my mother it was because Joey wouldn't sleep alone, but that wasn't true. It was me who couldn't sleep—not on Thursday to Sundays anyway. Having taken shifts in a local bar on those days, Mum left us with Gordon. Sometimes he would go out and *prop up the bar* as Mum called it, but over the course of several months he would stay home more often.

Locked in my concrete jungle, You seemed distant. They hadn't left me, I still sensed them at times, but I knew that You felt as stifled in the flat as I did, so I couldn't blame them for staying away. Only fear and depression reigned there.

It was almost funny. I was too young to really understand what romantic love—proper love, not childish crushes—felt like, yet I already understood what inappropriate, sleazy desire was.

Despite being curious about makeup, after our first proper experiment with it, I refused my mother's offer to buy me my own. She stared at me with abject disappointment. Finally, I was reaching an age when having a daughter could have been fun, yet I was denying her the chance to go shopping, get our nails done, and talk about boys who I thought were cute. Little did she realise the equal measure of disappointment it caused me to say no. I had gazed in the mirror and seen someone else—someone with possibilities beyond those four walls—but one look from Gordon, and I knew what he had seen and it made my stomach twist.

There and then, I vowed to stay in long sleeves and trousers, with my hair tied in a messy bun, and zero makeup on my face.

It worked for a while.

Joey had been poorly for a few days. Apparently uninterested in being a nurse, Mum had told both our schools that we were sick so I could stay home and care for him. Exactly where she went, I do not know, but as she started her shift at five in the afternoon and she left at ten in the morning, I know it wasn't work.

Exhausted from tending to a very grizzly little brother, my heart sank when Gordon came home with sunken, rolling eyes and blotchy skin. As a method of sobriety, I often thought that Gordon should take a photograph of himself whilst drunk and pin it to his second pint. Any later would have been pointless because by the time he reached the bottom of the fourth or fifth, nothing was going to dissuade him from drinking. I was sure that Mum must have fallen for him before she saw Gordon in that state as absolutely no one could love the demonic expression that inevitably took over him. How many drinks Gordon had had that day, I wasn't sure, but the moment he shut the door, it was obvious that he was in a mood, so I retreated to my bedroom and curled up beside Joey, desperately hoping that he would be quiet.

He wasn't.

After ten minutes, Gordon slammed the bedroom door open. "If you don't fuckin' shut it, I'm going to fuckin' shut you up," he snarled through gritted teeth.

Of course, Joey heard this, shook with fear, and started crying louder.

Clenching his fists, Gordon stepped towards the bed and my entire body trembled as I softly said, "Please, he can't help it."

Gordon chuckled. "Either he shuts up or you give me a distraction." As he spoke, his left hand grabbed his belt buckle and with a self-assured glint in his eye, he whipped it from his waist, cracking it for effect.

Joey squealed and Gordon lunged for him. Instinct took over, and I threw myself between them, screaming for Gordon to get out.

"Get out?" He laughed. "This is my fuckin' house—and you're gonna pay rent." He grabbed my hair and dragged me from my brother. Joey, bless him, tried to defend me, but with one shove Gordon sent him flying to the pillows and swiftly pulled me out of the room and into his.

Throwing me onto the bed, Gordon unzipped his trousers. I tried to run, but he lunged for the belt he had just dropped with expert speed and sent it cracking across the back of my knees. It would have hurt in jeans, but in cotton pyjamas the pain sent me to the floor.

Even though drunk, he was a million times too strong. Kneeling over me, he ripped at my clothes and touched me in places that made me want to die. Just as he was about to insert himself into me, I flung back my arms, reaching under the bed for anything that I could save myself with but nothing was there. My ears were ringing with the sound of my own pleas, but as if from nowhere, I heard a rustling sound and something solid rolled into my right hand. Grasping it, I brought it forward with every drop of energy I could muster, when suddenly Gordon's shoulders flew backwards as You dashed him across the room. The distance was perfect. As the baseball bat swung, the end caught Gordon's jaw, knocking him out in one swipe.

You whispered in my ear. There were no words, but I knew what the sound meant.

Dropping the bat, I left the room without turning back. Shutting the door, I heard the glorious chorus of You practicing their batting skills, and I knew they had hit a homerun.

———

Mum was furious. Her shrill cries were heard by the neighbours on both sides and they knocked on the door, calling out their concern until she came to her senses long enough to hear them. Gordon was in a mess but not dead. He wouldn't be able to urinate comfortably, let alone anything else, for quite some time and his face was swollen beyond recognition.

Joey and I were questioned in earnest. Did we not hear anything? Why did we not help? Joey answered first. I was anxious as hell, but I didn't need to be. It was a shame that it took such a hideous event for us to truly bond, but he lied with such perfection that I was proud to call him my brother after that day.

We could have told the truth. Of course we could. Or at least we could have tried. But it would have been pointless. I had already tried to talk to Mum about Gordon's wandering eyes and carefree hands, but she always laughed at me. To a normal, decent human being it should have been ridiculous. A man in his forties should not look at a fourteen-year-old girl with anything other than paternal or protective regard. Yet my mother saw and heard what she wanted to. Listening to the tales of her disgruntled children only ruined what she had worked for.

No, instead we told the story of a sick little boy sleeping in the arms of his loving sister, totally unaware of any horrors outside. The neighbours listened with charmed eyes as Joey spoke but I felt the twitch and twist of air as You circled them. Where were they when I screamed for help?

After an ambulance took Gordon away, my mother stayed to pack a bag. I stood and watched as she tried to mask her fear with chatter, but her shaking hands gave her away. Only when she went to leave did she truly look me in the eye. She paused. Her eyes glazed and her lips trembled as they registered the bruise that was slowly but surely rising across my face. Had she stripped me then, she would have seen the rest.

She didn't need to.

She understood.

But she said nothing.

A SULLIED TEEN

The lack of a shed had never bothered me more than during the following six weeks. My bedroom was not safe. No where was safe. As soon as I heard that Gordon was returning home, I emptied my wardrobe and set up camp inside. There was only room for a blanket and single pillow, but Joey and I squeezed ourselves in there every evening with Gordon's baseball bat firmly tucked up beside us just in case. If Gordon noticed his bat was missing, I do not know, he never came looking for it, but we jumped and trembled with each footstep outside our door anyway.

School was no comfort. It had been for a while after You taught Kimberley Jenkins a rather public lesson. No one spoke or touched me for weeks. It was bliss. Lonely, but bliss. However, returning to school with barely faded bruises emboldened Kimberley's spite and although she kept her distance, my locker and chair began to fall victim to her again.

A drawing of my death—so kindly labelled just in case I was in any doubt of the artist's intention—was left hanging in my locker. As I stood there, holding the paper, a hand laid on my shoulder. My entire body recoiled from the unwanted contact and a small, yet significant squeal past my lips.

While laughter erupted in the hallway as Kimberley and her friends rejoiced at their victory over me, I wanted the picture to come true.

"What's up Cassie-o?" grinned Kimberley. "I just wanted to see what you've got there?" She peered at the paper as though the subject were unknown to her. "Well, that is probably your best yet!"

My body and soul just felt heavy. Dirty. Gordon had beaten the fight out of me. Coming up with snide responses or even praying for You's intervention was beyond me. Kimberley saw it, and I glanced upwards just in time to see the light behind her eyes ignite. Her arm rolled back theatrically before her fist raced forward, landing in the centre of my stomach.

Doubling over in pain, I coughed and spluttered.

"Cassie-o!" Kimberley exclaimed with forced sympathy. "You should be more careful! Miss Keets—Miss Keets! Can you help? Cassie seems to be injured."

Miss Keets trotted around the corner as Kimberley swiftly removed her picture from my hand and scrunched it into a ball. My body froze as the teacher placed her arm around my back. Sensing my discomfort, she released me but hovered her hands over my shoulders. Even that felt like too much. Ducking away from her, I ran until I was clear of the school grounds and hoped I would find somewhere to fade into oblivion.

Having wandered aimlessly for hours, I headed to the flat to find Gordon in his bedroom and Mum asleep on the sofa. Perched next to her were two empty beer cans and her mobile with a flashing blue light as though it had a notification. Drunk or not, Mum often missed calls because she insisted on keeping her phone on silent. If ever mocked for it, she would always reply with: *Bad news will find me when I'm ready and good news will leave a message.* Perhaps she was right, but I had a feeling that this time bad news had also left a message.

Creeping to her side, I took Mum's phone and a knot formed in my stomach. She had a missed call from my school plus a voicemail notice. With little thought, I stepped into the hallway, listened to Miss Keet's request *for a little chat about Cassie,* and called school using the most mature voice I could muster.

Listening to Miss Keets' concern, I didn't know whether to laugh or cry. She clearly didn't know my mother any better than she knew me and had no idea she was waffling to a fourteen-year-old girl. Had Mum been in receipt of this news, she would have cursed, shouted for my immediate presence, and demanded an explanation—saving any true coarseness for later, but her tone would have been passionate nonetheless and anyone with an ounce of care might have read in between the lines. Instead, I calmly thanked her for checking in, made up a tale of a difficult menstrual cycle, reassured her that all was well at home, and that Cassie—*I*—would be absolutely fine tomorrow. Had I more faith in Miss Keets I might have sought her confidence, but like most adults she only truly heard what she wanted to—or had a habit of making things worse.

Returning inside, I silently slid the phone next to Mum and tip-toed into my bedroom as though I had stolen the family jewels. Tucking myself into the wardrobe, I felt the air twitch around me, and I knew the only one I could count on was You.

———

The next morning, I awoke to the sound of Mum and Gordon screaming at one another. It wasn't the first time, but their anger had intensified—or rather Gordon's anger had. His standard mood became so angry, so violent, that even Mum couldn't fake her way to contentment.

When Mum announced that Joey was going to stay with Trisha, Darren's sister, I instantly knew that I wasn't going too. Before his death, none of Darren's family liked me. I was the progeny of the enemy. The fact I was just a child and their son had taken over part of my father's business and married my mother was neither here nor there. At best, I would have been a stain on their family record to tolerate, but being the last one to see Darren alive cemented their hex on my existence.

The look on Joey's face as he left both lifted and sunk me. He was relieved for himself—I'm not saying he was thrilled about living, even if only temporarily, with his brash aunt and her family, but he knew it was the safer option—however, in his tender eyes I could see fear for me.

Alone in the cupboard, I hid from Mum and Gordon's raised voices and smashed glasses. Even times of relative peace were extremely strained, so after Joey's departure I remained out of sight for another two weeks. One morning when the fighting was particularly loud, I hugged my bedroom door, trying to judge where they were in the flat whilst anxiously watching the clock, knowing that with each passing second I was ever less likely to get to school on time. I decided I could make it to the front door but having left my lunchbox in the fridge, I held my ground a little longer. It would have been easier to leave it, but after skipping so many meals to avoid Gordon, I couldn't face the idea of not taking anything to school with me.

Finally, Gordon slammed the front door, so I crept into the kitchen. Mum was on all fours, sweeping up glass, but she looked up as I entered the room. Her eyes were red and puffy and a line of blood weaved its way down her left cheek.

Gasping, I asked if she was alright but instantly regretted breaking the silence.

"Couldn't you have just stayed in your room?" Mum stared at me through her tears, and I knew that she didn't mean that moment. "We could have been happy."

Unable to answer, I opened the fridge, removed my meagre lunch, and left.

My skin itched and burnt as I walked to school. It felt alive—like it was separate from me, yet really bloody angry we were attached. The idea that I was at fault for Gordon's violent, rapist ways weighed heavy on me. With hindsight, it is easy to say that is ridiculous. Possibly even then I knew it—certainly, I felt and dwelt the injustice of it—yet the potential that my actions or presence were somehow to blame taunted me.

How I longed to hide at the bottom of our old garden and never be found!

As I walked, a storm raged within me. My ears buzzed and my stomach knotted. Exactly how I made it to school without imploding or jumping in front of traffic I will never know. Yet as I walked through the gates it was as though You had been waiting for me. A reassurance sunk into my being as I felt their presence—and it reminded me of the joy I used to feel when I saw my father leaning against the red brick wall of my primary school. He'd have his truck keys looped around a finger, twirling them impatiently as though I were late, but he would beam and chuckle with open arms as I approached. No matter how angry he could be with the rest of the world, I was always safe in his arms.

A tear tumbled down my cheek as I remembered my dad, but as I went to brush it aside, You touched my face with an invisible force. My mind centred, and I smiled. You knew my thoughts. You cared.

"What's Jailbird smiling about?" I heard Lola's sarcastic snigger ring out across the playground.

"Hey, Jailbird!" called Kimberley. "I see you didn't understand the picture yesterday. Pity."

Instantly, my smile dropped but I could feel You twitching in the air around me. Wanting no part of their amusement, I hurriedly walked into the school building and into the toilets, barely stifling a groan as I heard the door swing behind me.

There were ten minutes until the morning bell rang. *I just have to survive ten minutes,* I repeated to myself.

The cubicle door rattled. "Jail-bird! *Oh, Jail-bird!*" sang Kimberley.

Four girls sniggered and cackled like witches as they continuously rattled the door and shouted obscenities. Frustrated by my lack of response, one of them grabbed a mop left by the cleaner and jabbed at my feet. Narrowly avoiding the handle slamming into my ankle, I quickly sat on the closed toilet with my legs hunched in front of me while the taunts continued.

"How'd you get those bruises, Jailbird?" Kimberley wasn't giving in. "Daddy can't have beaten you this time. What happened? Did you not give your client a good blowjob? You'd think you'd be good at it. Your mum must have taught you well by now."

"No, but yours did." The words just came out of me. I didn't fully understand what I was saying at the time. It was just filthy banter I'd heard, but with each insult I became less afraid and more bitter.

"What did you say?" The venom in Kimberley's voice was sharp enough to cut.

"Cheeky bitch," Lola snapped.

The bell rang.

"Come out and say that." Kimberley thumped the cubicle door.

"We'll sort this later," Lola said. "Come on or Miss Keets will be on us again."

There was a moment of quiet and all I could do was sit and try to listen over the racing sound of my heart.

"Come on," repeated Lola.

"Fine," Kimberley said with gritted teeth.

The door creaked as it opened and shut behind them. Distrusting the silence, I waited. Without crawling on the damp floor, I could not bend down to see if the room was void of feet, so after a few minutes, I took a deep breath and opened the door.

Immediately, Kimberley jumped out from her hiding position against the next cubicle and bounced in front of me with aggressive delight. I'll never forget the grin—the forceful grin of determination—that spread across her face. She set her jaw and curled her fist, hurling it into my face.

"Take that, you filthy bitch!" she said, pushing me with both hands into the open stall.

My feet stumbled, and I slumped into a heap, but as she went to kick me, I kicked out first, squarely catching her in the groin. Everyone knows that is a foul move on a guy, but that day I learnt it can be equally effective on a girl.

The air twitched as You revelled in my defence. I felt them jeering me on and lending me strength as the mop rolled to me. Grabbing it, I jumped to my feet while Kimberley spluttered. Keen to strike again before she recovered, I whacked her across the back of the head as hard as I could.

Her face turned to me as she coughed. A strange mix of loathing and fear oozed out of her.

Hatred filled me.

I swung again, and she screamed.

Slamming the mop on the floor, I shouted, "Enough, you fucking ho. Just leave me alone, right?"

A bully to the core, Kimberley spat on the floor as she stood up. "Jailbird's going to prison."

My heart sank as I considered if my actions were jail worthy. What was happening to me? All I wanted was some peace.

Suddenly, You held my arms. There was no noise beyond laboured breathing, but it was as though my invisible friend was whispering to me.

I've got this, You said.

The room felt dark. I knew I needed to leave. Nodding my head, I straightened my glasses, picked up my bag, and walked away with the sound of Kimberley screaming escorting me down the hall.

Kimberley didn't come to class for another hour. When she did, her leg was twitching so much I could see it from the other side of the room. Her hair was wet and scraped back into a ponytail, not loose like she normally wore it, and her lip was fat. As she sat down, Lola asked her what happened, but Kimberley didn't answer.

When the lunch bell finally rang, I nervously collected my things, hoping and praying I would make it out of the room before they spotted which direction I ran. Reaching the door, I heard one of Kimberley's group, Janie, ask if they were going to *finish up with Jailbird.* A morbid sense of curiosity held me outside the classroom door, waiting for the answer.

Nothing could have prepared me for it.

"I'm done with that skanky bitch. She's off her head—probably high since birth thanks to her skank mum. I don't want to waste any more time on *it.*"

Running to the top of the playfield, I smiled all the way.

When out of sight, I sat on a log and ate my bashed-up sandwich, profusely thanking You for whatever act of violence they had just performed.

———

Three days later, Mum instructed me to collect Joey from primary school. I wanted to ask why, but the sound of Gordon coming out of the bathroom was enough to scare me out of the apartment without further discussion.

Despite the fact I was late, Joey cried with joy when he saw me walking towards him. We didn't say much as we made our way home and neither of us rushed, but a silent appreciation for each other was definitely felt. Once at the flat, I anxiously opened the front door, hoping to find it empty—or at least peaceful because returning Joey to that house of horrors felt unkind and selfish.

The moment we stepped inside, Gordon's bedroom door swung open, banging against the wall. We both jumped and Joey's sweaty little palm squeezed my hand tightly while we waited to see who was there. As Mum's slender figure hastily appeared, looking flustered but not angry, my heart skipped with relief.

"At last," she said, dragging a bag into the living room. "We're moving. Grab a bag and carry it to the car."

Neither Joey nor I waited to be asked twice.

We didn't even ask where we were going.

Anywhere had to be an improvement.

It had to be.

———

When Mum parked in front of the hairdressers, I couldn't hide my confusion. I knew that Dee lived next to the salon and that she and Mum had been friends for years, but I had never envisioned living there.

Downstairs contained a modest living room, bathroom, kitchen, and walk-in-closet. Upstairs was another bathroom and four bedrooms meaning Joey and I had separate rooms. By my age I should have been grateful for this—we both should—but I looked around the empty space and felt lost.

Hoping for a garden, I leant out the window, but there, again, was none—just soulless roof tops and walls of the neighbouring buildings. For a moment, I despaired, but then my mind returned to the closet, and I felt the embrace of You telling me that, for now at least, it would be home.

Dee was a short, voluptuous woman with a bubbly personality and was definitely not afraid to tell my mother *I told you so* regarding her past relationships. To my surprise, Mum took her admonishment with flirtatious ease, and I quickly began to worry. Not because I was afraid of my mother being bisexual—that couldn't have bothered me less—no, I was much more concerned by Hal, Dee's husband. He worked away a lot, but I knew that we would soon be heading for another sofa in another town when this affair inevitably blew up in Mum's face.

For a few months I kept my concerns to myself, but realising that flirtation had spilled into a relationship, I tried talking to my mum.

She laughed at me.

"Sullen teens!" she declared, waving her arms above her head in feigned despair. "You can't cope with your old mum having a bit of a love life, can you?"

Remembering her prior accusation, somehow blaming me for her romantic woes, I walked away, returning to the closet and shut the door. Joey was already there. Neither of us were afraid of Dee, but we were afraid of the world. Joey would grow up faking his smile and I hiding mine, but together we were safe.

You was with us.

We never spoke of You, yet somehow, on some level, I knew that Joey understood that we were not as entirely alone as the rest of the universe would have us believe.

Each year I would sit my exams and pray the next term would see me in a different class, but Kimberley Jenkins followed me like a bad smell. If asked, she'd probably have said the reverse about me. She and the other girls had boobs now. Together they all wore bras, painted their nails, dated boys—or girls—and lived a youthful existence without once considering inviting me. Kimberley stuck to her word and although her seething hatred remained along with continued taunts and sneers, no one touched me.

I had officially become the 'it' that no one wanted to catch.

Although I knew it would take years of endurance to get to university, that seemed like my only window of opportunity. If I stayed in town and worked or got an apprenticeship, I would remain at the mercy of my mother. Only extended education would buy me a ticket from this hell.

Yet I looked at my brother and feared for what would become of him if I left. With an eight-year age gap between us, it would be the best part of a decade before he was self-reliant or old enough to come to me. Being the youngest and a boy, I had hoped he would be alright, but since Darren's demise, I too often caught my mother staring at him with the same regret that she bestowed upon me. He was growing, changing, forming opinions—and reminding her of a dead man.

My father wasn't dead, but in some ways he felt dead to me. I had stopped asking my mum to visit him years ago because there were only ever two responses to the question. The first and most consistent one was anger. She was very vocal about that one. In her eyes Dad had wilfully abandoned us and every error in her parenting skills was solely down to him. However, as time went on and my young, affectionate heart would not let go of the possibility of seeing him or at the very least sending him letters, Mum changed her answer. *It is a waste of time. He will not see you nor reply to your letters. I doubt he'd even read them. Your father's wishes are clear. He has left us money but wants no further contact with his family. I'm sorry, Cassie, but please stop asking for the Sun when I only have the Earth.*

That night, I wrote the last part of her speech in my diary. *Stop asking for the Sun when I only have the Earth.* I contemplated those words for hours—so much so that each year I inscribed them on the back page of my diary as a constant reminder.

It would take a very long time to see any error in that message.

Regardless of my mother's lack of wisdom, I did stop asking about my father. Uncle Gary, my only link to Dad, had long since tired of his protectorate role, so I decided that even if what Mum said was true—Dad didn't wish to hear from me—I would continue to write him letters with diagrams of plants and creatures. The only difference was I stopped attempting to post them. They became diary entries. If my mother ever went through my scrapbooks, I couldn't tell you, but I learnt to order my thoughts through writing without actually writing about the heaviness of the day. The sky was blue, the rain wet, coursework completed, and exams passed. Nothing about You or the true state of my emotions, but the act of quiet reflection gave me a glimmer of order in my otherwise freefalling existence.

When Miss Keets announced she was taking an extended break and Mr Yates was taking over as head of our class, I was somewhat indifferent. In his forties, Mr Yates had black hair with streaks of grey betraying the youthful look that he attempted to portray. Although mostly an English teacher, he was well muscled and certainly practiced what he preached regarding the body being a temple. It was a shame that he didn't extend that belief to his mind.

I had spent a very long time establishing my quiet spots in various classrooms. Kimberley may have stopped her attacks, but I knew which seats gave me the best chance of staying out of her direct eyeline. Trial and error had also highlighted who I could sit next to without incurring scowls—or outright jealous venom should the teacher require we work in pairs.

Mr Yates either didn't understand or didn't care for teenage social hierarchies, instead opting on day one to seat us all alphabetically. It could have been worse, I suppose, because I could have been stuck with Kimberley herself, but the instant I realised that my *Reilly* and Nic's *Reid* placed us together, I knew I would hate Mr Yates' reign.

Nic politely smiled as he pulled the chair next to me from under the table and ran his fingers through his ear length hair as he sat down. Were he arrogant about it, I'd have called the action preening, but I came to believe it was a nervous twitch more than a statement of attractiveness. He was though—attractive, I mean—not that I would ever have considered letting him know that. Nic was in the *in* group and Kimberley had an on-off relationship with him. The glare we received from her for daring to have surnames similarly spelt was enough to keep me meekly in place and not risk the ceasefire we had. I would, however, have preferred that someone other than Nic had a front row seat to my meltdown. Scratch that, I would have preferred not to have *had* a meltdown.

Mr Yates wore a different colour check shirt with dark blue jeans and trainers every day—although his tie was always the same bright red with his teams' symbol at the bottom. For hygiene's sake, I hoped he had more than one, but either way he would sit at the front of the classroom running his fingers down the fabric while he spoke as if someone had told him it was a good luck charm.

All the boys in my class thought he was fun and most of the girls had a crush on him despite his brash ways—maybe because of them. He spoke to us like adults when it suited him and shouted over-familiar banter when it didn't. He openly liked the loud kids and had little time or understanding for the odd girl at the back who really just wanted an hour or two to pass without being noticed. Perhaps he thought that booming at me would jump me into animation as he tried to explain the finer details of Macbeth, but when I didn't immediately answer his question, he loomed over me, boring his blue eyes into my soul.

Instead of my mind finding the answer, it took in his eyes and replaced them with Gordon's whilst whisking me to his bedroom as he pinned me to the floor. The blood rushed from my face, and my legs began to twitch. Mr Yates noticed and reached out his hand, making my skin burn as his fingers grasped my shoulder. Flailing, I screamed to the point I wasn't sure if I would ever hear another noise beyond the amplified sound of my own fear.

The room was a blur, yet sense told me where I was—in class with what felt like a million eyes staring at me. Attempting to run, the room spun, and I vaguely remember my knees collapsing before the lights went out.

My mother was suitably unimpressed when the school nurse called her. "Kids get excited, they faint," she said. She was even less amused when the school counsellor suggested therapy might help.

Mr Yates anxiously sat in the corner, probably fearing for his career. He didn't need to worry. No classmate would support me and my mother was never going to press charges for shouting at me—nor would she send me to therapy for fear of unpacking what she had taken pains to hide.

Dee offered to take us all to the cinema to relax and although I was reluctant at the time, I actually enjoyed a family meal and movie—or the closest thing to it—and honestly thanked her when she suggested that I work in the hairdressers as a cleaner at weekends.

I'd never become rich sweeping the salon floor or scrubbing the sink, but listening to Dee gossip with her clients while Joey played in the window seat was nice. When I finished, I would still collect my pastels and crayons and settle into the bottom of the closet, keeping half an eye on where Gordon's bat was hiding just in case, but it was the nearest to relaxed at home I had been for years. So, despite my reservations regarding their relationship, I had to admit that Dee was good for Mum. Or perhaps, more honestly, good for us all.

The threat of Hal returning home was always there and when he did we all kept out of the way, hoping that he wouldn't take offence at the lodgers his wife had taken in during his absence. From the closet, I heard Dee telling him how lonely she was and how our rent money helped buffer her income. He sounded unconvinced, yet as he was only back for a week or two at a time, he tolerated our presence and then flew off again under the conclusion of *we'll see next time.*

On my sixteenth birthday, I walked out of the school yard musing on what kind of cake Dee had made me. She had been teasing me about it for days and although I was fairly sure it would involve chocolate, I really wanted to see what design she had come up with. For Joey's birthday the month before, she had made him a horse shaped cake and taken him for riding lessons. He loved it and it soon became clear that this was the start of a lifelong passion for him.

Assuming that I was walking myself home as normal, I was about to step on the path to head away from the carpark when I heard a horn blare. Turning, I saw no one I knew—or who cared to know me—and carried on.

The horn blew again, this time longer and followed by a familiar female voice calling *Cassie! Hey! Cassandra!*

Glancing around, my eyes set on the waving arms of my mother as she leaned out the window of a campervan.

Following her bidding, I approached, but stood, gawping when I saw the state of her face. Her mascara had stained around her eyes, mixing oddly with the puffy, red and purple blotches as bruising flushed across her face.

"Are you alright, Mum? What happened?"

"Nothing. Get in," Mum replied, nodding to the passenger seat.

"Mum, who did that? Did you see Gord—"

Mum curtly waved her hand. "No. It's nothing. Get in." Her eyes refused to meet mine.

With no real options, I cautiously walked around the campervan, opened the door and climbed in. Joey was strapped into a seat behind Mum; his face a mixture of confusion and amusement as he tucked into a packet of sweets. I wanted to laugh—if only my fears where so easily distracted.

"Happy birthday, Cassie," Mum said. "What do you think of our new home?"

"Our what?" My eyes boggled. "What about Dee?"

"Hal came home."

Pausing, I let her words sink in. "Oh, I thought he was—"

"We were in bed." Mum rolled her eyes. "His bed."

"Oh."

Rage hit me.

"Did Hal do this?"

Silence.

"Mum?" I reached out, gently laying my hand on her arm as a teardrop weaved its way down her cheek.

Brushing the tear away, Mum forced a smile. "It's a new start, kids. Just the three of us. We'll stay in this until my friend, Fred Forde, has cleared out a static." She wanted to sound carefree, but a mirthless chuckle left her lips as she sighed. "Lucky I bought this last month, hey? I thought we'd holiday in it, but this is better, don't you think?"

Although I didn't hate her in that moment, I couldn't give her points for pre-empting the exposure of her adultery. I also couldn't understand why a house wasn't an option.

"Can't we rent or buy a house? Doesn't dad send money for—"

"We don't need a house—nor what your father thinks relieves him of duty."

For a second I began to panic that either he had reduced or cut payments, or Mum had somehow lost or refused my college fund. My getaway fund.

Lost in her own thought, Mum dismissively waved her hand. "Besides, that is tied to your education and food. I'm providing, okay?"

Glancing at Joey, I knew that neither of us were convinced, but I smiled and said, "Sure, Mum, of course."

"Let's get going," Mum said, turning on the engine of the ancient campervan. "We're going to park up at Fred's later, but I promised you a cake, so you'll have to go get one."

"I thought Dee made one?" Disappointment and reality hit me simultaneously.

That cake was never coming my way.

"Just jump out and get a cake—a big one—and whatever bits we might need for a day or two. Drink included—ooh, get me a bottle of gin." Mum waved her hand. "No, beer, twelve at least."

"Mum, I'm sixteen, not eighteen. I can't buy alcohol yet," I said, sliding out of the campervan.

"Shit, yeah, of course not." I could see Mum internally lamenting that I was still not old enough to be truly useful to her.

"Can't you come in?" I suggested in my least confrontational voice.

Mum scoffed. "With a face like this? I think not. The whole bloody town will be talking about it if I do."

Joey unclipped himself from his seat and took my hand, telling me he would help select the right cake. As he was the only one truly willing to spend time with me on my birthday, I didn't argue. I thought he brought his school bag out of habit, however, as we walked in the shop, he pulled the rucksack off his little shoulders and said: "Hey, erm, I drew this for you. Happy birthday."

Joey's blue eyes twinkled as he sweetly presented me with a birthday card made from an inverted cereal box. Whole heartedly, I thanked him as I accepted the picture, and found myself staring at it before going to sleep—kept up by the haunting sound of my mother quietly weeping. There, as though caught in a strange time warp, was our old vine-tangled flint and red brick shed. Joey had drawn a baseball bat leaning against the wooden door and placed an enormous shield in the grass in front of us both as we ate chocolate cake in medieval armour. Knowing Joey's obsession with *Dungeons and Dragons*, no one else would have considered a greater meaning behind his card, yet I could not stop looking at it. The shield, which had '16' written across it, really absorbed me. Sure, it was part of a knight's attire and the card was for my birthday, but the numbers were engraved into the cardboard with such thick, swirling black lines, I knew Joey had included You in our family portrait. I also knew I would keep that card until the day I died.

A NEW JOB

The novelty of living in a campervan wore off pretty quickly. Mum claimed the only bedroom meaning Joey and I were on the pullout sofa with all of our belongings boxed in the car or unceremoniously shoved into draws. I got up early the next morning to search for my things only to conclude that Mum, despite her claims to the contrary, had left my stuff behind at Dee's.

"It's not like I had a lot of time, Cassie," she said, running her fingers through her greasy hair. "I went back in the afternoon for our things but—"

Mum stopped talking.

She didn't need to finish.

Sitting at the little table, I glanced at the spot where I had displayed Joey's birthday card and sighed. I needed my things—my art equipment, course work, Gordon's bat, plus some of Joey's toys were in that closet. Turning back to my mother, taking in her bloodied and bruised face, I knew I couldn't ask her to return to Dee's.

A plan came to me. It was Saturday morning. Normally I helped Dee in the salon on a Saturday morning.

"Did you get my pushbike?" I suddenly asked.

"Yes—it's on the back of the van. Why?"

"I need to go to the library."

"Now?"

"Yes, if that's alright?" I said, crossing my fingers behind my back. "Do you need—"

"No, no, go." Mum looked out the window. "I've a splitting headache. I'm staying here for a bit. Be back early afternoon though. I told Fred I'd introduce you."

"Sure, no problem," I replied, checking the time. I'd be late, but I would go to work.

———

The caravan park was on the edge of town, and I hadn't taken into account how fast the cars would whiz past me as I attempted to complete my retrieval mission. Three cars sped past me like rockets and fearing for my life, I began to consider going back. Searching for a safe spot to turn around, another car came perilously close, and I closed my eyes as impact seemed inevitable. The driver must have swerved last second because I felt the swoosh, then felt the force of the grassy verge as inertia sent me tumbling to the floor, however, rather than my own life flashing before my blacked-out eyes, Mum's swollen visage filled the darkness.

Anger raced through me as I got up and swung my leg over the saddle of my bike. "Fuck you!" I shouted to the car who had disappeared beyond the horizon. Pushing off, I felt You rustle up a strong autumnal breeze behind my back. They had not left me. They pushed me along, and safely delivered me onto Dee's street before I had time to consider what I was going to say.

"Cassie, honey, what are you doing here?" Dee asked as I walked into the salon. She glanced anxiously at her client, Vera, before continuing. "I didn't think you'd be—"

"I'm here for my things, please," I replied, examining her face. Her normally shining eyes had dark rings underneath them and the corner of her lip was broken and surrounded by a deep bruise. My skin itched. She looked much better than my mother, but obviously Hal had shared his displeasure with both women.

"Your mum took everything, Cas—"

"Not from the closet, she didn't."

Dee forced a chuckle as she again glanced at her client. "Ah, of course, I didn't think about your hidey-hole when I packed."

My skin bristled. Mum said she packed alone. It could have been a slip of the tongue, but something told me it wasn't. Instinct—or dread—told me Mum didn't return for our things at all. She had them flung at her.

"How is your mum?" Dee kept her tone light and unassuming, but I saw terror in her eyes. "She hasn't called for—"

"Can I go in?" I asked, unable to cope with this charade any longer. "I'll show myself in." I walked towards the door that connected to her house.

Clearly panic stricken, Dee checked the time on her phone as I grasped the door handle.

"I won't take long. I'll be gone before you know it."

"Aren't you working here anymore, Cassie?" asked Vera as she watched me in her mirror. "I like our little chats."

"Sadly not, Vera, sadly not," I replied. Sweeping up hair, folding towels, and making ladies endless tea and coffee hadn't really appealed to me at first, but I had to admit that I enjoyed the banter with Dee's customers. Nothing I enjoyed ever lasted long though, so its demise had been predictable.

I left Dee to explain—or lie—about the reason for my departure and slipped into the house without another word. The house was eerily quiet, and any sense of homeliness was already null and voided as far as I was concerned.

Pulling the old cord, I switched on the closet light, and paused to say farewell to yet another home. Neatly stacked against the far wall behind a row of coats, mine and Joey's belongings were as we left them. Bending down, I opened up my rucksack, and hoped everything would fit inside. This wasn't a trip I wanted to do twice.

Deciding I would have to carry my coat, I rolled up Joey's and stuffed it on top before struggling with the zip of my bag as a shadow cast across the room. Gasping, I spun around to see Hal leaning against the door frame.

"What are you stealing?" Hal sneered.

Curling my lip, I matched his disgusted expression. "Nothing."

"Then what is in the bag?"

"My things."

"Your room is empty. I watched Dee empty it. What are you stealing?"

Again, Dee, not Mum. If Mum was there to take her things, why didn't she pack? I'd never particularly liked Hal, but knowing he was being cheated on by his wife, a part of me had felt sorry for him. In that moment, taking in his dark aura, I felt only hatred towards him. He was angry, of course he was angry, but beating my mother and his wife to a pulp made him the villain, not the victim.

It also meant I needed to get out, fast.

My options were limited. Hal was blocking the exit, and I had too far to run to surprise him and nip past his legs without him grabbing me.

"Are you simple?" My lack of response was infuriating him. "What. Are. You. Fucking. Stealing?"

"Nothing!" I bent to pick up my bag, grabbing my blanket which I planned to tie to the outside of my bag. In doing so, my fingers felt the hard, smooth form of Gordon's baseball bat as it lay hidden underneath. Freezing my body to the spot, I turned my head to face Hal. "I am only collecting that which is ours. This was our spot, for a while, you know?"

"Talk to your ho-mother about that." Hal's fists clenched by his side. "Despite your past family connections, I let you stay under my roof and she defiled it! Filth. That's what your family is—*filth*."

The lines of Hal's shadow twitched. You was warning him.

But Hal wasn't done. His face was red, his temples bulged as he spat out his words. "She deserves every mark on her. I should have kept punching and done you a favour by removing that fuckin' bitch from the—"

Hal didn't get to finish his sentence.

You started swinging.

The campervan rocked on its ancient axles as I entered. Embracing our new lifestyle, Joey was on the driver's seat, clutching the steering wheel whilst pretending to escort us to some imaginary land. Inwardly I thought it was a shame he had no such powers, but after watching him attempt to change gear, I hurriedly checked that Mum had had the sense to remove the keys from the ignition before Joey decided to test his real-life skills against his fictional abilities.

"Where's Mum?" I asked, glancing around the van. "In her room?"

"Nope," Joey said.

"Bathroom?" The shower box with a sink and toilet in it was hardly a bathroom but it seemed as easy to call it one. Joey shook his head. "I thought Mum wasn't going out? How long have you been alone?"

"Mr Forde came. She said they were having *a chat*."

A cold shiver struck across my back as I prayed the chat involved clothes.

"You got our stuff!" Joey declared as I unpacked my bag.

"Yeah, come put your things in a drawer. Mum doesn't need to know where I've been. We'll just say I found these things in the boot of the car after all."

Joey grabbed his action figure from the sofa, then paused with his left hand over another as it laid next to Gordon's baseball bat.

"Is that blood?"

"Paint," I lied. "One of my pots tipped next to it."

Joey chewed on his lip for a moment. "Did you see Hal?"

"Yeah."

"Did...did...y—"

The door swung open. "Ah, Cassie, excellent, you're back. Come meet your new boss!"

———

The caravan park consisted of twenty static caravans in an ornately kept field. Each one had a red brick border and wooden ramp-cum-balcony surrounding it. No one had a garden as such, but everyone had free access to the area around their home—and almost everyone had claimed a patch for either flowers or vegetables.

We were the only young family and the residents eyed Joey and me with suspicion—daring us to be loud or destructive so they could complain to Fred Forde, the owner, and have us evicted. As they glared at us, I wanted to tell them that my mother was loud enough for all of us.

Mr Forde was a thickset, but not fat man in his early sixties. He had brown, neatly kept hair, and wore pressed trousers and a casual, yet smart shirt and walking boots. His accent couldn't quite decide whether it wanted to be posh or not, but I soon found out that would vary even more depending on which side of his business you were presenting yourself as a customer.

The caravan park residents were privy to his more relaxed, colloquial tongue, but should you travel through the woods to the neighbouring holiday park, you would receive upmarket, high-end tones to match the significantly increased prices.

"You're to clean the lodges at weekends," Mr Forde said to me as I followed him through the trees. "Your mum said you've cleaned before and are good at it?"

I wanted to drop a sarcastic remark, but I bit my tongue and simply replied, "Yes, that's right."

"Excellent. There are six lodges and six glamping huts."

"Glamping huts?"

"Bespoke shepherd huts that we let out to holiday makers. We have a campsite too, but people pitch their own tents. We just have to pick up any trash they leave and keep the shower and toilet block pristine." Mr Forde stopped on the woodchip path and turned to face me. "Pristine. Not okay, near-enough, or anything else you care to come up with. *Pristine.*"

"Got it," I replied, arching my back away from his leaning face.

"Wonderful!" Mr Forde's face lit up and the corners of his eyes crinkled as he smiled. "It's such good timing as Fran, my wife, is too sick now and my daughter is due our first grandchild next month so she really does need help."

"I'm sorry your wife is ill. I hope she soon feels better."

His face dropped. "It's cancer—terminal."

"Oh, I'm so sorry, I didn't know." Internally I swore at Mum for not mentioning that essential detail. "That's awful."

He nodded. "It is. Thank you."

"Does your daughter live here, too?"

"Freda? Yes, yes, she and her fella live in Top Lodge with us and my boy, Freddie."

Inappropriate laughter threatened to bubble out of me. Fran, Fred, Freddie, and Freda Forde? Couldn't they think of another name? Instead I said, "That's nice, having family together." I wasn't sure if I meant it, but it seemed like the right thing to say. "Especially with a family business."

"Of course. Freddie helped me build the huts. We're carpenters by prior family trade. I've still got a workshop I tinker in, you know?" I wanted to ask how I'd possibly know that but I remained silent. "We've had lodges for nearly two decades but my son wanted the huts." Fred grunted. "Didn't stop him running off to college though."

"Oh, what is he studying?"

"Design and business. Got his brains from his mother."

"That's nice."

"Huh. For you, maybe."

Confusion bolted across my face. "Me? How so?"

"Your mum says you'll need a ride to school. Freddie is going to take you."

My blood ran cold. I hadn't even met this person and now I was being carpooled with him. When married to Dad, Mum had lots of friends, then working in bars and restaurants for years, she met people easily, but how she fell into so many laps and favours *so* quickly baffled me.

Why she couldn't discuss anything with me first, frustrated the hell out of me.

A NEW RIDE

Swinging the campervan door open, I scanned the space for my mother and found her propped up amongst the cushions Joey and I were using as pillows.

"Hey, Cassie," she said weakly, holding the back of her hand against her forehead.

I probably should have been more concerned about her pale countenance, but I was still angry about being so quickly palmed off onto yet another person. Why couldn't she—*my mother*—for once take care of me herself?

"Why can't you give me a ride to school?" I snapped without introducing the subject.

"Excuse me?" Mum attempted to narrow her swollen eyes.

"Mr Forde says his son is driving me on Monday."

"What is wrong with that? It makes sense. I am working here or in the opposite direction, Freddie is driving your way. I don't see—"

"I've never fucking met him!" I squealed, slapping my hands against my thighs.

"Don't you fucking swear at me!" For a millisecond I saw Mum register the irony in her rebuke, but she brushed it aside and carried on. "When he was showing me around, we got chatting about logistics. I mentioned dropping you off at school, Fred said his son was out at that time and could take you, so I gratefully said yes. I suggest you do the same." She scoffed. "Joey is going with you, too—"

"Do we even finish at the same times?"

"I'll pick you up most days but, if need be, you'll go collect your brother on foot and wait wherever Freddie tells you to." Mum sat up. "Stop scowling. Don't mess this up for me—*for us*. I'm trying to land on our feet. Can't you see that?"

A tear rolled down my mother's cheek and the fight left me. I wanted to curtly reply that she always landed on her feet somehow—or her back, but my inner voice told me that was unkind and try as I might to totally hate her, I loved my mother.

Instead, I tried a topic change. "Could we not live with Uncle Gary? He has so much space and did offer—"

"No. Absolutely not."

"I don't understand. I—"

"I thought we'd moved past all the Gary talk." There was no question. Just a disappointed statement.

"You got on okay most of the time and he—"

"I don't want you living there."

"Why not?" I was almost pleading.

"We left that life behind." Mum sighed. "Maybe you were too young to see it."

"See what?" Encouraged by her softer tone, I carefully sat on the edge of the sofa by her.

"Did you see the basement at Gary's?"

My mind flashed to the beautiful annex Gary offered me, the large house, the garden, but no, I hadn't seen a basement. "I don't think I knew there was a basement."

"Well, there is. A big one."

"What is down there?"

"A large chunk of the old family business which we no longer want part of." Mum's tone was tired and cold.

"The men who came and went were workers—Dad's crew?" My mind felt like dawn was rising, but along with it a certain amount of trauma was resurfacing. My demons would not stay buried. Mum was declaring Dad and Gary's business beneath her, yet she had profited from it—continued to profit from it—for over two decades. Darren had continued it and lost. She moved away. Perhaps she did want a fresh start, perhaps friends of old had seen her wavering loyalty and been less than supportive, but either way she had thrown herself and her family from one frying pan to another. In my gut I could feel the fire. "They wouldn't have harmed me. Gary wouldn't have let them. They were loyal. Dad had included me—"

"*And then left us.*" Mum grimaced. "Sure, with money, but also a noose around our necks. A crew with no strong leader is rife for disloyalty and attack. You revere the memory of your father but he may as well have left us for dead in the dirt. Cassie, you don't understand. I wanted to start again. I went where I thought it was safe—"

The air around me shook. "*Safe?*" The word tasted like toxin on my lips. We stared at each other, eyes darting in pained disbelief, defiance, and deep-seated disgust. Unable to articulate how hideously wrong she was, I jumped up and stormed out of the campervan.

A breeze pushed my curls into my eyes, and I suddenly felt hugged. Wiping the rising tears from my eyes, I sighed. "Thank you, You," I whispered. "Only with you do I feel safe."

———

Walking through the woods, I heard my brother giggling. The sound cheered me but I also felt bad because I hadn't considered where he was during my altercation with Mum. Creeping around a large oak, I found my brother standing beside a man cleaning his truck.

The man looked mature but young—I guessed in his mid-twenties, but later found out he was actually only twenty. He had streaky blond hair scraped into a ponytail and two-day stubble. Joey was clearly relaxed in his company and his laugh was gentle, but You bristled around me as we approached, and bristled again when the man's cheeky dark eyes sparkled in my direction.

"Hey, Cassie, come meet Freddie!" Joey said enthusiastically. "We're going to ride in his truck on Monday!"

My brother's joy was undeniable. He was willing—longing—to move on and forget our past woes. Joey equally wanted and needed this move to be one of happiness. Unlike me, he had friends at school. Whether any of them knew the truth I don't know. I doubt it because he hid his angst the moment he left whatever door we were calling home at the time. Here was no different except the door led into open, green space and a man that could be a big brother. A big brother who liked to make stuff and could drive.

It was jumping ahead massively to suppose all this so soon, but I could see it in Joey's eyes. The hope. It simultaneously warmed and froze my heart. I wanted to reply, "No, we ain't getting in that bloody thing," but instead, I smiled and said, "Oh, really?" in a slightly playful tone. For my brother, I would play my part. Or at least try to.

Freddie dried his hands on his trouser legs and stepped towards me. I won't lie. He was gorgeous. The only trouble was he knew it and the last thing I wanted was to be at his mercy for a ride—to school or so-called home.

"Hi, I'm Freddie," he said, extending his right hand.

"Fred *Junior*, I'm assuming?" I replied, shaking his hand lightly so I could back away easily.

Freddie laughed. "Yeah, but please call me *Freddie*." There was that twinkle again.

The air twitched around me but I didn't need You's warning. I had no intention of becoming a notch on this guy's post or pandering to his ego—no matter how much I enjoyed being regarded with something other than confusion or disgust by anyone remotely resembling one of my peers.

"Can we go for a ride now?" Joey tugged on my arm.

"No, Joey, we cannot. Monday will come soon enough." Addressing Freddie, who had returned to his vehicle, I said, "I am sorry you've been lumbered with us."

"Nah, you're good. Our parents have been mates for a bit. Your mum's working, I am driving out." He shrugged. "Makes sense." Freddie looked me up and down. "Can't say I mind."

Joey was beaming, but neither he nor Freddie made my anxious heart relax.

———

Riding in Freddie's pristine truck made me nauseous. He had obviously inherited his father's love of tidiness but as the smell of aftershave mixed with polish I began to worry for the longevity of the vehicles' cleanliness. Joey was overjoyed to be driven to school and despite how green I felt, I couldn't ignore the difference in his demeanour. With sadness I thought it was a shame that our mother couldn't witness this alteration. She never would though. For attached to her was a shadow—a net of memories combined with a desire to please her that made us so anxious neither of us could truly relax in her presence, no matter how hard we tried.

"You could tow a pony trailer with this thing," Joey announced, dragging my attention back to the present.

Freddie laughed. "I guess I could."

"Do you ride?" Joey beamed hopefully.

"No, I never tried." Freddie saw Joey's face drop. "Do you?"

"I did. Dee used to take me, but since Mum and her broke up…"

"I see." Freddie glanced at me. "How about you, Cassie? Are you a horsey-girl?"

His focus returned to the road, but I could see his eyes flicking back to me, waiting for an answer. I couldn't decide if his question was out of genuine interest or the runner to a joke. If at school I would certainly have been walking into a joke which I was the butt of.

"No." Short and simple.

"Cassie watched me—and helped me groom Lupin." Joey said proudly.

"Lupin?" Freddie chuckled, raising an eyebrow suggestively at me. "I'm hoping Lupin's a horse."

I rolled my eyes but Joey didn't notice. Instead, he proceeded to spend the next five minutes telling Freddie all about Lupin and how perfect he was. Truthfully, he only stopped talking because we arrived at his school. I wanted to get out at that point because without Joey to centre my thoughts, my mind started to race and it felt like a dark force of scurrying mice was running back and forth inside my head.

Logic told me I only had five minutes alone with Freddie and he had done nothing to suggest he wasn't trustworthy, yet logic had been replaced by fear of the uncontrolled, making the large truck begin to feel hideously small. Silently, I begged You to find me. To hold my hand. But this new form of terror blurred our connection. I was alone—and sweating horribly. By the time we arrived at my school, I barely managed to utter thank you before scuttling into the nearest toilets to throw up.

Hostility seemed like my best form of defence. Answer when spoken to but give nothing away that I didn't have to. I worked when I was told to, I studied when I had to, and spoke only when spoken to—which was frankly more than I cared for—but when free from all of the above, I wandered into the woods and felt the presence of You as they walked beside me.

We still had no shed and now my bedroom was smaller than Dee's closet. When I pointed that out, Mum was quick to remind me of my love of small spaces. "This should be like heaven to you!" she declared as we moved from the campervan into a static caravan—two weeks later than originally promised. I said nothing, but wanted to point out there was a big difference between a small space I escaped to compared to one I was locked in with her. When I realised Mum had no intention of selling the campervan, in the hope of securing something resembling a hiding hole, I asked if I could sleep in it and leave her and Joey in the caravan. That idea was shut down immediately.

"We live under one roof," she stated. "Small or not, we stay together."

"I'd only be two meters away and Joey could have his own room," I tried to reason.

"No." Mum turned up the radio. Discussion over. Once sure I understood her point, she rubbed her head and reduced the volume once more. "Darn headaches," she muttered to herself.

She wouldn't admit it, but the frequency of her headaches was becoming impossible to ignore.

Scrubbing toilets was not a vocation I enjoyed but, as Mr Forde so cheerfully pointed out, I did it well. So well in fact, my mother decided I could help her during the week when she was behind. Why she was behind I could not understand. Fine, sometimes customers were late leaving or special arrangements had been made. That might explain the occasional alteration to routine, but Mum's work patterns became more and more unpredictable. The only thing I could predict was when being collected from school: Freddie would be on time. Mum would not.

One such day, Mum was half an hour late. I had already collected Joey from his school and started walking home. Together we had decided it was better to keep moving and hope she would find us before we reached the long, speedy road that led to the caravan park.

Most people had disappeared in the opposite direction, but ahead of us on the path was a girl from Joey's school. She stopped to tie her laces just as a white car pulled up next to her. At first I thought it was someone she knew as she seemed relaxed talking to them through the window. Then I saw the passenger door open and a hand holding a bag of sweets.

The hair on the back of my neck immediately stung with icy fear. "Do you know that car?" I hurriedly said to Joey, pulling him into a faster pace. "Something's not right."

"That's Ursula," Joey replied. "Her mum has a black car."

"Hey! Ursula!" I shouted and the little girl with beautiful dark brown curls turned to me. She stared at me in confusion until she saw Joey, then smiled. "Who is this?" I asked as kindly as possible through hastened breaths.

"I—erm, he—" Ursula glanced at the man.

"I'm just taking Ursula home. Her mum asked me to collect her today." The man spoke quietly but confidently. Like what he was saying was the most natural, harmless thing in the world. "Come on honey, we better get going." He patted the passenger's seat.

Ursula's eyes spoke of her confusion.

"Where does she live?" I asked.

"Excuse me?" A flash of irritation marred his smile.

"If you know Ursula's mum, you won't mind telling me where she lives."

"I can't go giving out people's addresses to strangers." The man scoffed but suddenly a new smile crept across his face. "I can give you a lift home too, though, if you like? It's going to rain soon."

If he knew how many times I had walked or stood in the rain in my life he would know why my immediate reaction was to laugh. Instead he looked offended and his expression transported me back to Gordon. Evil, angry, rapist, Gordon. He pulled on the sleeves of his black jumper, then adjusted his beanie hat, and got out of the car. As he opened the rear door for us, his eyes seemed to shift and it felt like he was calculating his next move.

You's shadow suddenly felt like it was engulfing the car. They were warning me. We had to get away. I took both children by the hands. "Thanks, but I will get them both home."

"It's fine, I'm here now," he replied, taking me by the shoulder. "Let's go."

Panic set in. Outrunning him wasn't an option, so my eyes darted for something to attack with. His fingers dug into my skin, and I wriggled to free myself as he pushed me towards the open car door.

Resisting his direction, we tussled until my ankle twisted and thrust my body forwards, landing me hard onto my knees, simultaneously smashing my face into the inside of the open door—making my glasses feel like they had been impaled into my skull. Dazed, I became aware of a warm trickle of blood running down my forehead as the man grabbed Ursula and swung her into the front seat over my back.

"Stop!" shouted Joey, hitting the man as hard—but ultimately weakly—as he could.

"Get in, boy," the man said, forgoing all former pleasantries. As his bony fingers dug into my arms, I reached for the door and You popped open the glovebox, revealing a hunting knife.

"Run!" I screamed at Joey and Ursula. Both dumbstruck, neither child moved. Still fighting for control with the man, I screamed again, "At least get back!"

Barely registering their compliance, I swung for the man. Screams increased and combined as bodies knocked and thumped into each other and up against the vehicle. The man's hands clenched around my wrists, but despite the blur of jarring, painful movements, I held firm. Adding to the array of cries, wheels screeched to a halt behind me, a door opened, and suddenly I was dropped as my attacker was yanked sideways. Now released, my hand thrust out one more time and felt like it had lodged into the tyre.

Words roared around me but my head rang so much I couldn't decipher them until Joey's voice broke through and echoed in my ears.

"Cassie! Get up, Cassie! Please!"

Rolling onto all fours, I attempted to push myself onto my feet. Sensing my struggle, You lifted me, releasing me as both children ran into my aching arms. Trying to register what was happening, I saw Freddie smashing the man into the side of his vehicle. They wrestled, throwing as many punches as they could get in. Dazed and outmatched, I could only watch, hoping Freddie could best our attacker. For a moment I thought he might, but suddenly Freddie took a hit to the face which knocked him back just long enough for the man to jump into his car and speed away with the passenger side doors flapping in the wind.

Having checked them over first, Joey and Ursula silently sat in the back of Freddie's truck while he used a wad of tissue to stop the bleeding on my forehead. We'd both need a bag of peas on our faces that night. All still out of breath and in shock, I was glad my fear of being touched was numbed just long enough to allow me to be helped.

"Thank you," I whispered to Freddie as the police arrived.

The cheeky grin had gone, but his melancholic smile somehow still seemed sweet as he replied, "You're welcome."

While the police questioned Freddie, he lamented not having arrived sooner, and I found myself questioning why the victims are always left blaming themselves when there's only one person at fault?

My ears were still ringing, but when a voice came over the policeman's radio, the news cheered my weary soul and cleared the fog long enough for me to rejoice at You's skill.

"We've arrested the assailant," said the police officer on the other end of the radio. "Did any of the victims mention a knife?" The officer with me confirmed that I had. "Clever—or lucky, I suppose. It punctured the tyre." He chuckled. "The car crashed into a lamp post right in front of me."

THANK, YOU

My mother displayed a suitable level of distress when she collected Joey and me from the hospital, but once alone she quickly rebuked me for walking up to the car in the first place. No remorse for not collecting us on time, no regard for the little girl who was about to be abducted, or apparent pride that I had stepped up even when terrified. I tried to tell myself it was her way of showing that she cared but honestly it was a hard pill to take.

It wasn't until we got home that I noticed she had driven Mr Forde to the hospital. At first, it seemed sensible so father and son could drive home together in Freddie's car, but something was off. They arrived too soon—and Mum wasn't wearing work clothes.

Waiting until Joey was asleep and she had a glass of wine in hand, I leaned against the kitchen cabinets and said, "Mum, are you dating Fred?"

Her eyes shot up to me but she said nothing. Last month, I found her scrolling on a dating app and she gleefully told me she was going on a date with someone called Martin. As her absences had increased, I had assumed that she was still seeing him, but in that moment, staring into her eyes, I saw the truth.

"He is married, Mum." I spoke gently but my words thinly veiled a reprimand.

"I know." Bowing her head a little, Mum put her wine glass on the coffee table. "I know." She patted the sofa. I sat down. "This is going to sound awful..." She waited for me to respond. I nodded, indicating that I was ready for whatever she was going to say. "But his wife is as good as dead."

I was wrong. I wasn't ready.

"What?" The word snuck out of me without me opening my mouth.

"Their marriage was just like a friendship before Fran got sick. Fred has cared for her diligently and the end is near..." She paused, fidgeting with the hem of her skirt. "I'm hoping that after we might have a future. Maybe, anyway."

"And you can't wait until *after*?" I asked, using air quotation marks.

"I don't need your sarcasm, Cassandra." Mum sneered. "This place could be part of your inheritance if we play this right."

Everything was a game of cards to my mother. Every meeting an opportunity. Some you bank, some you discard, some you take a chance on and play out your luck, but absolutely everything and everyone were part of her game of life. I very much doubt she managed to shake a single hand without simultaneously considering if the acquaintance wouldn't benefit her at some point.

The fact Joey and I could have been taken, abused, or murdered that afternoon while she was spread-eagle was just another way the cards fell. Freddie saved the day. Another card well played. Another hand well shook. Never mind who got hurt in the meantime.

Standing beside the swimming pool with a cleaning kit in my hand and apron around my neck, I wondered if the water felt as trapped as I did. Did it long for the sea? I decided not. It always had the hope of evaporation. Sure, the clouds might be turbulent, but there was always the excitement of landing somewhere new. To finding the sea—*home*—next time.

I had no such hope.

No one was going to beam me up.

The sound of slow-moving wheels on the path snapped me out of my musings. Coming towards me was Freddie pushing his mother in a wheelchair. Immediately, my mother's cruel words came to me, and I had to agree that this woman did look like she was reaching the end of her life. Sorrow hit me in the stomach—and guilt. If my mother felt none it was apparently my burden to feel it for the both of us.

Forcing myself to smile, I nodded politely and started to walk in the direction of the glampers shower room.

"Hey, Cassie," Freddie called after me.

"Hi," I replied, retracing three steps.

"This is my mum, have you met?"

I hadn't. Despite being onsite for months, I had only seen Mrs Forde from a distance—usually when she was bird watching on her porch, and I was hiding from my mother in the woods. "No, I've not had the pleasure." I'm sure I learnt that response from a film, not Mum. "It's lovely to meet you, Mrs Forde."

"Fran, please!" she replied warmly. "I've heard a lot about you, Cassie."

"Oh?" I glanced worriedly at her son but he just smiled. "That's rarely a good thing in my experience."

Fran chuckled and despite my confusion, I relaxed. "All good, I assure you. Although, your recent ordeal was hideous." She pointed to my bruised face. Apparently active pain was necessary to understand her as my fingers automatically reached for my cut, making it smart.

Gazing at Freddie, I saw his matching purple bruise. "It would have been much worse if weren't for your son."

"I'm very glad he drove by when he did." Fran smiled up at Freddie. "I'd rather you weren't in danger, but I'm very proud of him for stopping that awful man."

There. There was the reaction of a normal mother. A good mother. "You should be." My voice cracked as I spoke, and I had to gulp hard to restrain a misplaced sob. I needed to walk away as my mind again felt like a deranged creature—knocking into the sides whipping up sadness and anger as it went. "It was nice to meet you," I said, stepping away, "I'd better get to work. It's a lovely day for a stroll, I hope you enjoy it."

Freddie was uncharacteristically quiet, but his mother spoke out, apparently not yet done with me. "Can someone else do the cleaning today? I'm sure you need some time off."

This woman is going to make me cry, I thought to myself, forcing a chuckle. "I don't think the couple in the third hut would agree with you. They texted your husband three times yesterday about toilet roll when it hadn't even run out!"

"Yes, he said." She laughed. "But they can wait. What do you want to do when you're older, Cassie?"

My eyes must have boggled as my ears took in her question. A simple question. A common question for a teenager about to sit her GCSEs. A question no one except my disinterested teacher had previously thought to ask me. In my most sarcastic voice, I nearly answered, *Does it matter?* But something stopped me. Possibly it was her tired, weak appearance; perhaps it was the notion that my mother was rude enough to her for the both of us; but I honestly think that her warmth of spirit overrode those things, and I just liked her. So, for the first time, I answered truthfully. "I like gardening. My dad used to teach me, so I think I'd like to take after him a little." Fran smiled, so I carried on. "I can draw, too. I think landscape gardening would be amazing."

"That's wonderful, Cassie. Are you studying for that now?"

The spell broke. "No. Mum wants me to do A levels, then university or a fulltime job. Then she says I can decide on a career."

"Oh? But you can study more specifically earlier, can't you?"

The truth was, I didn't know what my mother had in mind for me. University used to be spoken of favourably, but lately she told me that she didn't want me going away at eighteen. I was disappointed, but didn't want to leave Joey with her, so I didn't push it. It wasn't money—not unless Dad's funds had inexplicably run out. Watching my brother, seeing him succeed, had to be my vocation. Accepting my fate, I had already signed up to another two years in my hellish high school.

"Sure," I replied lightly. Tears rippled beneath the surface and threatened to expose me. Breaking down wasn't an option, so I made my excuses and left.

———

The ride to school that Monday was extra quiet. As always, Joey recovered from—or repressed—our trauma the fastest, but even he was distracted that morning. Mum had surprised us both at breakfast with mobile phones. I had always had a love-hate relationship with the desire to own one. Social media seemed like a waste of time—it was just another thing to get bullied on, so I was happy to give trolls one less bridge to hide under—but on occasion it would have been nice to call my mother or brother instead of hoping I'd find them.

If Freddie hadn't been there, even if I had managed to wiggle us all free from that man, I would have been left to flag down a passerby last week. I am almost certain that Mum's change of heart was directly linked to the police and social worker at the hospital pointing that out.

"I've put our numbers and Mr Forde's number on there. Calls, texts, that's your lot. I've restricted the data, so no streaming," Mum said with raised eyebrows, placing the phones on the table in front of us. "I will be checking."

In that moment, Joey's social life increased tenfold as his contact list soon filled with friends' numbers. Mine, however, remained exactly the same.

As I walked into class, eyes turned to me and bore into my purple bruise. News had obviously travelled ahead of me. Since his arrival, despite my meltdown, Mr Yates was still my form teacher and had never changed our class seating arrangements. It might have started by pure coincidence of surnames, but I did wonder if, over time, Mr Yates realised that Nic Reid's sitting next to me was just a safer bet—even if it did eternally upset the girls in our class.

They didn't need to worry though. Regardless of me being candid or not, any crush I felt for Nic Reid was firmly suffocated by their stares. Any and all conversation we uttered was strictly business-like. I knew better than to upset any apple carts and despite how long it was since a pin had been left in my chair, I still checked every day. Possibly by then *I was* the thorn on their blossoming roses. They certainly made me feel that way.

After a morning of silence, the bell rang and everyone chatted noisily as they collected their belongings to leave the room. I got up, ready to take myself off to the library to hide, when Nic said. "Thank you."

Tilting my head, I narrowed my eyes, hoping to make sense of Nic's remark. "What for?" I eventually asked.

"For saving my sister—Ursula."

"Huh." That was the extent of my intelligent response. Internally groaning, I forced myself to try again. "I didn't know she was your sister. How is she?"

"Shaken. Definitely shaken—but safe, thanks to you."

The unintended reality of his statement wasn't lost on me. Sure, Freddie and I played large roles, but it was You who found the knife. Yes, I thought. "Thank, You."

In addition to the mobile phones, Joey and I saw two further benefits following our attempted abduction—well, possibly three because Joey and Ursula became friends. Joey kept saying they were *friends with benefits* but I then had to sit him down and explain that at eight—or eight and a half as I was quickly reminded—children should neither know nor use that term. Inevitably it was then left to me to explain the more sexual nature of the expression. Joey's eyes widened as the birds and the bees were laid out before him.

"I just meant a little kissing!" he declared innocently.

"A little kissing is fine," I chuckled.

"So," Joey said thoughtfully, "maybe she's my girlfriend?"

"Maybe." His rosy cheeks made me smile.

A horn blared from outside. Mum knew it annoyed the neighbours but she did it anyway. Afraid she would revoke our plans, I said nothing when we got in the car. Finally able to disassociate the riding school and her time with Dee without bursting into tears, Mum was taking Joey back to his lessons. He was over the moon.

As we sat in the car, watching Joey go around and around the arena on a bay pony, Mum suddenly spoke. "We broke up, by the way."

My face spun to hers, searching for emotion that she was apparently unwilling to share. She wouldn't even take her eyes off Joey.

"With Fred—Mr Forde?" I asked quietly.

"Yes."

"Oh... That's good. I'm sorry for you, but, you know—"

"Yeah." Mum shook her head then rolled her shoulders as though she was about to start exercising. "We're starting something new, you and me."

Her change of tone worried me. "What's that?"

"We're doing self-defence classes."

Having had to defend myself too many times and always needing You's strength, this news pleased me. I had no intention of replacing You, but guidance, plus a little action—or release of tension—sounded good to me.

"I met the instructor yesterday." Mum turned to me and winked.

Obviously, I was missing something. "*Okay...?*"

"He's gorgeous."

———

Witnessing your mother flirt is rarely a pleasant experience for any child, but for me it was pretty soul destroying. I was now old enough to hear my mother's tales on dating—or what she wanted to do to the guy who just served us coffee, brought us our takeaway, or was teaching us how to deflect an attacker.

Never did it occur to her that all the acts she spoke about made my skin wriggle and writhe. It wasn't uncommon for me to wake up in a wet sweat but never in a good way. I took up running in the woods to *get away*. It was the safest place I knew and You ran beside me. Together, my anger would stream behind me, and in front was only trees and creatures of the woodland who neither cared nor bothered as I flashed past.

Mum was disappointed in my lack of interaction. I was disappointed in her lack of understanding. Two peas from vastly different pods—zipped together by fate, not by choice.

She was content with the dirt of the Earth, while I longed for the warmth of the Sun.

CAT AND MOUSE

One weekend, while Joey was away at pony club, Mum drove me down a dirt track to a field surrounded by enormous trees. I wanted to get out and introduce myself to the fauna and flora, but my mother was not interested in satisfying my quirky desires. I was there to learn to drive. My seventeenth birthday wasn't until October and Joey would turn nine first, but Mum was keen for me to prepare for my birthday early. "You need to pass your test as fast as possible," she said without explaining why.

Fearing I would be blamed for bringing on one of her headaches, I chose not to ask. I also chose not to ask how she knew of this glorious hideaway. The well-established tyre marks and makeshift parking bays on the left-hand side of the field told me more than I wanted to know—and ensured I never visited here after dark.

Sitting behind the wheel felt liberating. I shared my mother's desire to learn quickly, so on this one she would not need to beg or badger. Being able to take myself places would be a game changer. It had to be. Waiting for Mum in the rain was tedious, anxiously glancing in every car that pulled up was becoming an obsession, and hurriedly walking to find my brother so I could catch a ride with Freddie was frustrating. So yeah, I wanted to drive. Sure, Freddie was good for Joey and I sensed their natural friendship strengthening but his cocky tone unsettled me—and he knew it. He enjoyed it.

No, driving myself, being in control of my own destiny, was the thing I craved the most.

"We're going to the movies!" squealed Joey as I walked through the trees that separated the caravan park and Top Lodge, the Forde's house.

"Excuse me?" I blankly glanced between my brother and our chauffeur. "Joey, what game is this one?" Over the course of a few months, Joey had taken to trying to enrol Freddie and me in various games as we drove to town. Possibly it was his way of breaking the ice each morning—or more specifically, my ice, because I was the antisocial one, not Freddie—but if nothing else Joey's antics had proven amusing.

"No game! Freddie is taking us to the cinema—right, Freddie?"

"Joey, leave Freddie alone—"

"Actually, I did say I would," Freddie cut in, almost looking shy.

"That's sweet, but no, thank you."

"*Cassie!*" Joey was so frustrated he could only shout my name.

Freddie's all too familiar grin spread across his face, producing dimples in both his cheeks. It baffled me how he could seem twenty-five in one moment and eighteen in another.

"Well, I'm going to the cinema tonight. If you want to come, I'd love to take you both. If not, you can wait in my truck or get home another way."

We were already late leaving so I didn't have time to nip home and ask if Mum could pick us up later. I texted her on route but she obviously didn't read my message properly.

I put: "Can you pick us up from school tonight? Freddie is going to the cinema."

Mum replied: "Great! Have fun!"

Pretending I had some kind of say, I tilted my head, arched an eyebrow, and twisted in my seat to face Freddie straight on. "Is this film age appropriate for Joey?"

"It's Disney!" Joey exclaimed.

Now my brows really arched. "Whose idea was that? I can't believe it was yours, Freddie." His smirk was undeniable. "You're telling me *you* want to watch a Disney movie?"

"I've seen them all to date, so yeah, I do."

That bloody grin. I wanted to wipe it. Joey revelled in it. You wanted to smack it.

———

All day I tried to think of ways to get home that didn't involve miles in the rain, walking my eight-year-old brother down a verge-less 60mph road, or sitting in a darkened cinema with a boy who was four years older than me and clearly full of his own self-importance.

"You make me laugh," Freddie whispered into my ear while Joey filled his pick and mix bag beyond its limits.

His proximity made me shudder but I masked it by spinning on my heels. "Why?" His face was still too close.

"Because in the rare moments that you forget yourself, you relax."

I wanted to retort that that was the problem—*forgetting*—but I remained silent. I didn't know what else to do.

Joey returned with his sweet haul and we entered the cinema. As Freddie headed for the back row, I pulled Joey into the middle aisle, reminding him it was the best position for our necks when he protested. Freddie looked irritated but followed suit, and I expertly placed Joey in between us. My knees still shook though. I didn't know why, but I couldn't control them.

Anything but relaxed, I chain ate Joey's sweets until Freddie's fingers brushed mine in the bag, and I instantly felt the weight of my gluttony.

Freddie was an unreserved flirt. He did it for amusement, yet his eyes unsettled me every time—not in the way that Gordon's eyes bored lustily through me, but still enough to make me anxious. I couldn't decide if I wanted Freddie to be serious but I told myself he was not. I couldn't cope with anything else anyway. Had I any doubt of that, when he stretched his arm around the back of Joey's chair, his fingers stroked my shoulder, freezing my body. When he tried to touch my neck, my arm took on a life of its own as You brushed him aside like a fly had just landed.

Freddie chuckled.

This was a game to him.

A game of cat and mouse.

MOUSE TRAP

My mother loved the idea of a romance when Joey gleefully suggested it one evening. Neither of them could understand why I would be reluctant to pursue Freddie's flirtatious nature. I protested, pointing out that Freddie was not the type to have serious designs on me, but Mum simply argued that a little teenage experimentation was normal.

"So what if it doesn't end in marriage and happy ever after?" Mum laughed. "Go out, have fun. Kiss some frogs until you find your prince! You won't find him or her sat there."

Mum's words cut me. What was considered *fun and normal* petrified me to my core.

"I know there is an age gap, but what of it?" Mum continued. I suspected she was counting the years between her own *experiments*.

Desperate to change the subject, I decided now was as good a time as any to ask Mum if I could take over the little plot outside the caravan. "I was wondering if I could plant some veg or maybe different flowers there?" Mum didn't reply so I carried on. "I know George has been tending to it, but his knees are bad, and I was hoping to trial—"

"I pay George to do it," Mum cut in.

"Then I could save you some money!" I smiled, hoping to have found an extra reason in my favour.

Mum twisted her lips. "No, no I don't think so. Paying George was the only way to make any peace with the old hags next door. If I stop they'll start moaning about something again."

"Can't I just have a little patch?" I badly missed growing things. It had been years since I had been able to tend to anything other than an avocado stone—and that had been left on Dee's kitchen window ledge. If Hal realised it was mine, I doubt he left it in its jam jar.

"No, Cassie, I'm sorry. I like the patch as it is."

"It's so boring! Everyone's patches are the same. I could—"

"I said, no." Mum's face dropped.

"What about a new plant box? One just for me?" Her face was stern, and I was pushing my luck, but I had one last card to play. "Maybe as a birthday present?"

"It's not your birthday!" Joey unhelpfully chipped in.

"When it is," I added. I figured it could be something to look forward to.

Mum sighed. "Cassie, I'm sorry, but it's not my yard to be filling with plant pots."

Sorry was just a word for her. She wasn't even willing to ask.

"Ooh, maybe Freddie will get you some flowers!" Joey's glee spread to our mother but missed me entirely. His face beamed as he got the desired laugh from Mum. I wanted to hate him for it but understood why he was so pleased. Recognition and reward were hard to attain in our family yet making someone laugh achieved both of those goals.

"No, Joey," I said dryly. Picking up my jacket, I left the caravan without another word.

———

That weekend Mum took us into the town centre to get Joey new shoes. Unable to cope with my sullen face, she instructed me to amuse myself for half an hour and meet them outside *Marks and Spencer*. I knew they would take longer, they always did, but I went anyway.

Heading towards the nearest bookshop, I found myself unexpectedly captivated by a market stall selling plants. Despite most of my wages being claimed by my mother, I had money in my pocket, and I could have happily spent it there and then. However, I knew that without earth to call my own, even with the freedom of the sun, I would just be condemning the plants to die.

About to walk away, the wind rotated a display rack full of seed packets. Simultaneously, I felt You push me towards it. It was like the wind and the undefined being were defiantly forcing me to meet them in the middle. My hand reached out, gently lifting the minute seeds in their brightly coloured sleeves and my mind danced with ideas and patterns.

"Good choice," a voice said over my shoulder.

Turning sharply, my eyes met the kind expression of the elderly market stallholder. Blushing, I smiled, and went to replace my selections when the wind—or You—turned the rack round and away from the spot I needed.

"You could grow those almost anywhere," the man said softly. "Large or small, wild or homely."

It was like his words were chosen by a higher power.

Wild.

Where was I happiest?

"You're right!" I said, grinning. "Thank you, I'll take them."

Having paid the man, I left, still dreaming of the little spot in the wilderness that I was going to claim. Entering the bookshop, the air around me buzzed happily. I had found something that did not require my mother's permission. My only concern was that without a bag to hide them, I might have to explain my seeds. I wanted them to be my secret. My gift to nature that required no explanation.

We had little room for storage and Joey claimed more than half, so what I read was mostly digital, however, I had a few physical gardening books which I protected against my brother's encroaching possessions. That day I proudly claimed a new one and nestled the seed packets inside the dust jacket.

Having waited an extra twenty minutes, Mum finally arrived swinging two shoe boxes in separate bags. My heart thudded against my chest as I waited for her to inspect my purchase, but true to form, she simply glanced at the book, rolled her eyes, and declared it dinner time.

It took me another week to find time to wander deep into the woods but I took a small bucket from the cleaners store, filled it with fresh water, commandeered a trowel from the gardeners shed, and disappeared for three hours.

Joey was away with friends and Mum was either working, out with friends, or on a date—the lines between the options blurred so much that I didn't ask where she was going when she dressed up anymore—so no one noticed my absence.

My skills needed honing and tools improving, but I enjoyed every second of my time in the woods. The day was warm but not hot, the sun poked through the leaves of the trees, making beautiful patterns on the broken ground as the wind gently swayed the branches. I knew that an element of luck would be required to guide these seedlings into adulthood because I could not protect or tend them every day. It was possible that I was simply adding variation to the local rabbits diet, but that was nature's prerogative. My freedom was to plant—*and hope*.

———

Returning to the caravan with mud imbedded under my nails and brown patches on my jeans, I wasn't thinking about anyone. I certainly wasn't expecting to see Freddie leaning against my porch as I broke the cover of the woods. Had he not been staring right at me I would have retreated back into the trees.

"Hey," he said, casually pushing himself off the porch rail into my direction.

"Hey," I replied, suddenly conscious of how dirty I was. "Are you looking for Joey? Sorry, he is away for the weekend."

"Nah, not this time," he said, running his fingers through his sun-streaked hair. "Although he owes me a rematch at footie—the little tinker won last time."

Making up their own rules, the ball games they played were not true football, but they seemed to have fun regardless of any technicalities.

"Mum is out too..." It seemed unlikely Freddie wanted my mum, but no less likely than he had come around specifically for me.

"I was waiting for you." If You had feathers, they ruffled hearing that sentence. My friend was almost always with me now. I took comfort in their silent presence. I did not take comfort in their displeasure—especially as it mirrored my own. "Your mum said you were alone. I thought I would come hang out."

Instantly, I felt like a mouse again, staring down the barrel of a trap.

No words came to me, so Freddie spoke. "Where have you been?"

"The woods." Freddie looked me up and down, obviously questioning why I was dirty. "I fell over a log." My simple lie was enough to satisfy him.

"Would you like a pizza? I'm ordering takeaway."

My stomach rumbled, and I wanted to hit it for betraying me. Pizza was much more appealing than the alphabet soup and toast Mum had suggested. Suddenly, it dawned on me that she probably planned this. *Fabulous.*

"That's kind, but—"

"Oh, come on, Cassie!" Freddie said, pulling out his mobile phone. "You're hungry, I'm starving. Why can't two people eat pizza without fighting through barriers?"

Barriers. I found his choice of words curious but he was right. I lived my life with barriers.

You prickled around me, reminding me that my barriers were there for a good reason. Maybe the pizza was the cheese to get me to run into the trap, but maybe I was already trapped. All I had to do was find out whether it was friend or foe trying to catch me.

"Anything but Hawaiian, please."

"Ah-ha!" Freddie laughed. "A girl after my own heart. I knew it!"

BLOOMING HELL

It was no surprise to find my mother jubilant the next day. Telling her that Freddie and I just hung out and ate pizza might as well have translated to *we got married, had sex, and won the lottery*. Perhaps her joy came from the blind hope that her daughter was taking a step towards the normality she so desperately pleaded for. Part of me enjoyed her silly bustling, but none of what she fussed over was true.

We had sat apart, leaning against two trees, talking about film, sport, the weather, Joey, and his mum. The light was almost gone when he spoke about the latter. At first I thought Freddie was going to stop as his tone dropped significantly, but then he carried on with tender honesty. Happy to be a sounding board, I let him talk without interruption. It was the least arrogant, least cocky, I'd ever seen him. The jokes, the spirited, playful nothings that he was so good at were stripped back, and I almost relaxed in the presence of that version of Freddie. I could still feel You weighing him up, but even they had been quieter than normal.

"How did you part?" Mum asked eagerly, folding her legs underneath her as she sat on the sofa.

"We said, *goodnight*." I couldn't resist using a slightly sarcastic tone.

"Very funny." Mum tutted. "You know what I mean."

"Mum, I can't tell you what didn't happen. You want me to tell you some romantic gesture took place. Nothing happened." Disappointment struck my mother. "It was *not* a date."

"He must have said something!"

"Yeah, *see you later*." Actually, his sister had called asking for help as his mother was feeling rough and her baby was screaming uncontrollably. Before he left, Freddie asked for my phone number, but my anxieties immediately flared, so I made some lame remark and as he was in a rush, we said good night. Only Mum and Joey had my number. No one else needed it—but I was sorry for the look on Freddie's face when I said no.

Tired of her probing, I set off to work hoping the current glamping guests had left because I was fed up with scrubbing their mud off the walls. How they spread so much dirt, I couldn't tell you. I understood the floor. It had been raining, they went walking—that was a simple equation—but every day it seemed like they had been in a mud wrestling match and the toilet and shower walls were the umpire.

Hours later, when I was finally finished for the day, I went to check on my seeds. As I had not moved into a fairytale, it was impossible for any of them to have grown, but I wanted to see if any wildlife had disturbed the patch.

My heart skipped as I walked towards my wild garden. My seedbeds were untouched, but next to them, sticking out of the ground, was an empty pizza box. Cautiously I pulled the box from the ground and opened it. In black ink Freddie had written his number and the message: *If you won't give me yours, at least you can have mine.*

Although I ran straight into the house, found a lighter, and burnt the pizza box behind the caravan, I will not deny having walked home smiling. I will also not pretend that I didn't save Freddie's number before destroying the evidence—therefore saving myself from Mum's inevitable quiz—whilst silently repeating *this is for emergencies only.*

Mum had the following week off work so she drove us to school, meaning I didn't see Freddie. You and I decided it was for the best. My exams were approaching, and I couldn't afford any distractions. More importantly, I couldn't afford to fail. Every plan or idea of a plan I ever dreamt of involved me passing everything and escaping.

"I'm going to be late picking you up tonight," Mum said on Friday morning as we pulled up to the school gate. I wanted to add *again* but waited for her reason. "I'm not sure when I'll be done, actually. Freddie is busy—it's his twenty-first apparently and has some big party with his mates, and I asked Old Fred, but he is tied to his wife, so you'll just have to wait." There was a bitterness to her voice that worried me.

"Shall we start walking?" I asked, catching Joey's anxious glance. Neither of us where happy with that idea and still shuddered if a car, no matter how innocent, pulled up next to us.

"No, no," Mum said. "I don't want you walking down the main road. If the police see you they'll be knocking on my door again, telling me I'm unfit."

I stared at my mother. "Has that happened before?"

Mum waved her hand. "Just don't, okay?" She grasped the steering wheel again. "Go to the library. I think there's a club there after school?"

"There is." I knew that because I had desperately asked her to take me months earlier but Joey's riding lessons or meet ups with friends always clashed—or Mum just couldn't be bothered.

"I could get Ursula's mum to take me to hers?" suggested Joey.

"Ursula is visiting her grandmother." Mum had obviously covered that option too. "Just go to the library."

Until that day, I hadn't thought to ask when Freddie's birthday was. Apparently Joey knew as he then informed me that he'd drawn a card and popped it through his door that morning. It crossed my mind that I should text Freddie and wish him a happy birthday, but I immediately dismissed the idea as stupid. My skin rippled with goose bumps at the notion seconds before my angry side kicked in. If Freddie had wanted me to know about his birthday, he would have told me. To me, this proved I was just an amusement when he was bored.

Going out with friends, Mum had said.

So, yeah, not me.

Message received.

Relieved to have completed another week, I left the grumbles of my fellow students behind me in search of my brother. Only five streets away, it didn't take me long to get to Joey's school. He was pacing like a caged tiger when I arrived but he was just being impatient, not upset, because as soon as he saw me, he instantly smiled and redirected his march towards the library. On the way, he told me about his day, about his friends, and I was filled with gratitude that his school experience was so vastly different to mine. Possibly it was the luck of the draw, and he got better classmates, maybe his character was simply warmer than mine, but whatever the reason I was happy for it. Jealous, but also happy.

Finding a new fantasy novel, I curled up in one of the corner seats while Joey drew whatever weird and wonderful scene came to him. You no longer seemed to figure in his pictures—or at least less prominently. There was the odd, seemingly out of place dark rim that I spotted, but on the whole pictures were of football, friends, or horses. Not necessarily in that order.

Seeing my brother settled allowed me to relax, and I became so absorbed in the book I was reading that I could have fallen through the pages. When Mum rang, telling me she was outside, meaning we had to go, I wished I had.

Mum's mood was strange as we slid into the car. She was clearly tired, yet she forced a cheerful smile as she rattled on about who she had seen, the traffic that held her up, and the glass of wine she was longing for.

"Fuck it!" Mum declared, slapping the steering wheel with the palms of her hands. "Let's go out for dinner—a proper one!"

Watching her hands land on the steering wheel, my ears rang with a kind of white-noise, blocking out any further words. All I could focus on was the white hospital tag around her wrist.

When I failed to respond to whatever she said, Mum nudged me. "Earth to Cassie! Come in, Cassie!" I blinked, trying to take in her face. "What's up with you? Don't you want chocolate fudge cake?"

Worry for mine and Joey's future raced through my mind. *Joey*. I had to protect Joey. "Sure, I'd love cake." I giggled, and conversation carried on as though nothing was wrong.

Pulling up outside the pub, Joey bounced out of the car, declaring he'd beat us to a table. Mum grabbed her bag, then reached for her door handle when I caught her left arm.

"What is it, Cassie?" Mum asked, somewhere between concern and irritation.

I pointed to her wrist.

"Oh." Mum paused, then laughed, ripping off the tag. "Just women's check-ups! Don't worry, honey, I'm all good!" She laughed again. "Although being poked you-know-where was less than pleasant!"

Holding her gaze, I searched for the truth. "Are you sure?"

"Sure." Mum looked at me in earnest.

I needed to believe her but my mind and heart were racing in opposite directions.

"Come on before your brother orders everything," Mum chuckled. "Huh," she said, staring straight ahead. "Is that Freddie?"

Surrounded by more than a dozen friends, there was Freddie. All of them wore matching printed birthday shirts, streamers, hats, and goodness knows what else. It seemed that the party had started early with food and they were then about to move on to the next part of their night. Impatient for dinner, Joey returned to the pub doorway and tapped his foot in our direction. Spotting Joey's less than subtle hint, Freddie instantly called him over. Happy to be seen, my brother eagerly greeted the group, cracked some joke which everyone laughed at, then ran to Mum as she locked the car, appealing for speed.

"Who's that?" I heard one man ask Freddie.

"A sweet kid who lives in Dad's park," Freddie replied affectionately. Glancing back to Joey, he then noticed me and Mum. Still at a distance, we both said happy birthday to which Freddie smiled awkwardly.

Either not thinking we could hear or not caring, the friend followed Freddie's line of vision, asking, "And them? Who are they?"

"They're his family."

Not *a friend*. Not even *a girl I know*. Just *Joey's family*.

But that was right. Joey was everything. The least damaged of my family. The most likely to succeed—and I needed to protect him.

Mum's grin told me that she wanted to talk to the group, but I hastily wrapped my fingers around her arm, halting her movement.

"Let him celebrate," I said firmly, but quietly. "This is *our* family night."

Nodding solemnly, Mum used her free hand to squeeze mine as it laid on her arm.

"Quite," she said with an uncharacteristic sense of calm, leading us inside without looking back.

OVERCAST

Finishing my GSCEs was anticlimactic but I was relieved, nonetheless. I wanted to walk out of those gates and never return, instead I had to settle with a two month break and the joy of not hearing about the bloody school prom anymore. Mum was despondent when I refused to go. She had dresses she wanted me to try, makeup she wanted me to wear, and a hairstyle she was dying to try on me.

Yet I was still not the daughter she had hoped for. Her disappointment brought on another of her headaches—or so she declared—so all end of academic year celebrations were reduced to a cake and walk in the woods with You.

That was fine by me.

Dee, whilst with her, had joined forces with my mother and persuaded me to try on clothes that vaguely fitted me. I kept with styles that were by definition loose, but I did concede to wearing a size twelve instead of fourteen. Mum tried to tell me my true size in the clothes she selected was ten, but we'd never find out if she was right because I flatly refused to try them on.

Anything resembling tight clothing still felt like I was under attack, and despite Mum's suggestions, the idea of attracting attention to myself was exactly opposite to my desires.

Running through the woods at the furthest point of the property, I heard a wail. At first I thought it was an animal—maybe a deer—but then I realised the tones were much more human. Still distressed, but definitely human.

I was worried it was one of the campers in trouble. The previous month one of the families had lost a ten-year-old boy for two hours and everyone was beside themselves. He turned up, unharmed, having walked off *to teach his parents a lesson*. Furious her time had been wasted, it was perhaps ironic that my mother found him, but it was certainly colourful when she marched him home, angrily declaring what lesson she thought he needed to learn.

Approaching where I thought the sound was coming from, with the light now dusky at best, I saw the outline of a man. I'd avoided him as much as possible lately, but I instantly knew it was Freddie. His shoulders shook as rage and sadness struggled within him. There was no need to ask what had happened. I could tell. His mother had died.

You tugged on my sleeve as we stepped towards Freddie. *Let him mourn.*

With tears in my eyes, I walked away and for the first time in a long time, I allowed myself to think of my father. The man who didn't want to see me. The man who I had cried for just as Freddie was for his mother.

The circumstances were different, but I understood his pain.

———

My mother insisted that we attended Fran's funeral and seemed to take pleasure in dressing Joey and me up in black. She fussed over Joey's shirt and tie, and straightened my dress as though we were about to take a family photo. I say *as though* like I had experienced that, but I hadn't. We had family selfies, the odd picture stolen thanks to a willing passer-by, but no one ever organised a professional portrait.

"I don't want any makeup, Mum," I said as she came at me with her makeup bag.

"What, why not?" Her face was a picture of genuine surprise. *How has she not morphed into a proper girl by now?* it said.

"It's a funeral."

Mum chewed on her lip, thinking of something I might agree to. "What about straightening your hair like mine?"

"I like my curls."

Mum deflated, and then it hit me. Like I struggled with Joey's blue eyes, so she struggled with my curly hair. The reminders of absent fathers. Well, I had found a path to loving my brother regardless of his father. Why could she not do the same?

"I'll look like a member of the Addams family if you straighten my hair," I said, placing my hands on my hips.

A chuckle rippled out of me.

Suddenly, that seemed applicable.

Sitting down, I let her straighten my hair.

———

For Joey's ninth birthday, Mum took twenty children paintballing and then to pony club where she had organised a barbeque. It was a lot of fun—even if it was exhausting to the point of me needing forty-eight hours without seeing anyone to decompress afterwards. Mum swallowed paracetamol before the party started and I'm pretty sure it was the first thing she did when we got home, but I don't think anyone considered the energy wasted.

With that excitement now behind us, October brought the day that I had been counting down to. This was my day. My seventeenth birthday. I wasn't expecting a party like Joey's—honestly, it would have been a sad and depressing affair if Mum had attempted any such event. You and I were capable of celebrating my birthday in perfect silence which would not haunt my waking or sleeping dreams. Actually, my countdown was more closely connected to the fact my birthday landed two weeks before the half term holidays when I was booked to go on an intensive driving course. To say I was nervous was an understatement, yet with any luck, I would return to school as a licenced driver. I had to. Mum had continued to take me on our dodgy field drives, and I was getting good. Sure, I needed to practice in the real world, but I could emergency stop and three-point turn like the best of them by that time. Thanks to a couple of early-doors doggers, I had also learnt how to reverse park and accelerate quickly.

Doing A levels in the same high school was not my first choice, but Mum was not open to discussion. Just over a month into the first term, feeling as out of place as ever, I decided my birthday was a good day to try talking about another school or college again. Mum argued there was no sense in changing, I argued the opposite. She said being so close to Joey was too big of an advantage, while I said that once I can drive it would not be a barrier and new faces might do me good. Mum said I was odd wherever I went so it was better the devil I knew.

Deflated, I walked outside.

Immediately, the sound of my brother's bubbly chatter filled my ears. Having befriended George, the resident gardener, Joey was busily telling him about his latest sporting achievements with painstaking detail as the old man crouched over our flower garden. In no hurry, I stood and listened, hoping for some green-fingered talk with George if Joey ever stopped talking when Mr Forde and Freddie appeared through the trees. Seeing the men approach, I decided it could wait. Darting indoors, I called to Mum who was in her room, waited long enough to be sure that she was coming, and whipped out the door, around the far corner of the caravan, into the opposite row of trees, and into oblivion before anyone could think to ask where I was going.

Beyond where I had made my garden, there was an enormous oak tree. Its trunk was so wide, four people could hug it simultaneously and its branches twisted and curled towards the ground as though they were inviting me to climb up and rest upon them away from the eyes of the earth. The ground fell away into a valley just beyond the tree. Not so close the tree was in any danger of toppling in high winds, but still near enough that sitting up in the branches gave me the notion of surveying a little kingdom.

As the sun lazily shone through the woods, it occurred to me that building a shed—a small log cabin perhaps—and living far from the strains of humanity would be a pleasant way to spend my life.

"There she is!" declared Joey.

"Huh, so this is where you hide." Freddie's face peered up at me. I hadn't even heard them coming.

"There's a difference between hiding and retreating," I replied wryly.

"What's up?" Freddie asked, shielding his eyes from the sun.

Scoffing, I gazed into the treetops on the horizon. "Nothing new."

The sound of Freddie's feet scuffing the foliage below rustled its way up to me. Maybe he was waiting for me to expand on my own but I had no intention of continuing. As far as I was concerned, he either understood or he didn't.

"That tree is huge!" Ignoring us, Joey skipped around the tree like a carefree rabbit.

"Why have you two come out here?" My skin began to itch with irritation at being found.

"I hear it's your birthday?" Freddie wasn't really asking a question so I didn't reply. "Happy birthday."

I sighed. "Thanks."

"Do you have plans? I thought you'd go out with your friends?"

A dry laugh drifted out of me. "You have to have friends for that."

"I'm your friend."

"You're only my friend out here or in the dark," I retorted without thinking whether I wanted to say the words.

"They're the only places you relax," he said coyly.

Leaning forwards, my eyes shot down at Freddie.

He might have been right but neither You nor I appreciated being told.

"Cassie says she's going to drive soon," Joey declared. "*If* she passes her test."

"Thanks for the vote of confidence, Joe." Scraping moss from the bark of the tree, I threw it at him. Whether by default or design, he had a way of disarming my mood.

"Need a lesson?" Freddie asked, reverting back to his typical grin. "We could start on the back lane and see how you feel?"

My mouth wouldn't form words, but my lips pulled into a smile. Clutching the tree, I shimmied towards the ground. Freddie offered his hand to steady the small jump that was required, landing me right in front of him. Instantly the scent of slightly damp trees was overridden by the sweet, moreish aroma of his aftershave. If asked previously, I would have said I preferred the former, but honestly, he smelt amazing.

"So, is that a yes?" He smiled, chuckling.

"Yes," I said. "If you are sure?"

Freddie pulled his car keys from his pocket. "Your chariot awaits, milady."

Two weeks later, entering the driving centre, I shook from head to toe with fear. Between Mum and Freddie, I had practiced every day. I spent a week on the course as a nervous, shaking wreck, but I absorbed every detail given to me. Walking out, I still shook, but this time with a licence. I would only have access to Mum's car when she said so, but freedom was one stage closer. Cutting the chains of my childhood was closer. The scars would remain, but with each footstep, I felt You with me, and I thought back to Joey's card last year. The three of us would walk in the shade of the Sun, not the shadows of the Earth.

We had to.

NEW YEAR, NEW YOU?

Mr Fred Forde had Scottish roots so although he decorated around the park for Christmas, New Year was what he truly looked forward to—and the whole camp was set to benefit from his celebrations. Top Lodge, the Forde residence, was marginally set back from the main road and had a pebble track winding behind it. That path ran alongside the woods parallel to the caravan site, leading to the fields where the holiday lets and glamping huts stood. On the grass between Top Lodge and the holiday lets, Fred erected a marquee, set up a spit roast and barbeque, hired a bar and DJ, and rented three hot tubs. I didn't understand the latter as there was a swimming pool and two of the lodges had hot tubs installed already, but who was I to judge?

Everyone on site was invited and everyone who was invited seemed to have invited someone else—except me, of course. Joey had a gang of friends over including Lisa, his new girlfriend of two weeks. After a few months, he and Ursula had decided they were just friends meaning he was single until

Lisa had declared them together during a PE lesson. So simple. I was happy for him, he deserved to develop and test normal friendships during his childhood, even if seeing him so carefree and well-loved stirred extra solitary feelings within me. That was my problem, it should never be his.

After scrubbing things all day in preparation for the New Year's party, I stood in our bathroom, staring at my dry, sore hands. I didn't understand why Mr Forde was so keen on things sparkling when we were set to be largely lit by campfire, but I kept my mouth shut and did as I was told.

Deciding it was time to go, with one hand firmly pinching my elbow, Mum dragged me to the barbeque while Joey skipped ahead of us. "Eat up. Free food must be taken advantage of," she whispered as she released me. "Enjoy yourself!" she declared loudly as she walked away. "See you next year!"

Obviously, she had no intention of coming home that night and was happy to leave her nine-year-old son to run wild in a field and sleep in a tent of his choice when he was ready. It hardly seemed wise, yet the presence of other kids' parents and grandparents gave me some comfort.

Taking a burger, some crisps, and an orange juice, I walked away from the fire into the shadows of an ash tree and sat down with You beside me. Smiles and laughter accompanied the crackling wood until the DJ started his set. I preferred the more organic sound if I am honest, but despite myself I felt my toes bopping along to the beat. It was a relief that a part of me, however small, was enjoying itself because my eyes couldn't help registering how many cups and plates were being idly tossed onto the grass—and then calculating how long it would take me to clean up tomorrow.

Mr Forde and my mother were soon dancing. My insides groaned. How long, I wondered, would it take for her to try to redefine her status here? Old Fred was OK. His business was clean—as far as I knew—but Mum didn't wait for love or even true attachment or matching ideals before she jumped in. She only sought a warm bed, solid roof, and the slightest hint of affection and she would be all in without further thought. Caution or children be damned.

I'm not saying I wanted to stay in the caravan forever. I just didn't want to move into the house only to find myself living in the car. Again.

Yet whenever I urged reservation, Mum declared me a prude. I was always back to being the sullen teen who stifled her joy. Part of me wondered if she was considering leaving Joey and me in the caravan while she moved into the house. The way she acted that night could have been suggested as a trial-run. Perhaps only the presence of Mr Forde's children and grandchild were actually delaying her plans. If that was the case, I was grateful. He was Mr Nice Guy. He was the perfect host at a party, but too clean, too precise, for my haphazard mother. Distanced from mourning his wife, I was sure he would soon realise that, yet as he laughed and joked, it was also clear that he found her relative youth alluring. When he began to grab her buttocks with increasing zest and dance closer and closer, my stomach churned. The majority of the crowd wouldn't have noticed anything beyond a slow-ish dance, but I, facing Mum's back, had a prime view.

I had to look away.

My eyes landed on a group of people my age. It was a surprise to see them but I supposed they were family of the residents—many of whom had temporarily forgotten their dislike of anyone under fifty for the holidays and had joined the celebration. When I saw Freddie amongst them, I still thought nothing of it, especially as he had college friends beside him as well.

Where his father left off, Freddie continued to circulate, ensuring that all was running smoothly with the assistance of a tall, blonde girl. She held his arm, giggling, and a pang hit me. I told myself it was jealousy of her freedom, her unreservedness, but if honest, it was more. Or both. It felt impossible that I'd ever talk to anyone without cringing inside—or would ever touch anyone without burning.

You briskly rustled the air around me. This was the closest to touch I'd ever take without some element of fear—perhaps excepting my brother but including my mother.

The girl seemed familiar although I was fairly sure we had never met. It wasn't until she and Freddie returned to their original group, new drink and food in hand, that I saw why.

Another girl, slightly shorter, but otherwise remarkably similar turned to greet them and hatred bubbled within me. Why was Kimberley Jenkins here? Was there no way for me to rid myself of her shadow? No DNA test was required to answer the first question though. Of course Freddie had to be friends with Kimberley's sister—wasn't that just how my luck went? And gauging the state of my luck and the volume of alcohol in their hands, tomorrow I would be cleaning up their puke.

Checking my brother was still being overseen by more attentive parents, I retraced my steps through the trees and headed for the caravan. Approaching the end of the track, the sound of hushed giggles filled my ears, so I stepped off the official path, hoping to avoid them. Reaching the edge of the treeline, I came to an abrupt halt as my eyes caught sight of two figures fumbling under the porch light of our caravan.

Old Fred barely gave Mum time to open the door before he pulled her jacket off and undid his belt. Apparently, they had every intention of ending the year with a bang.

Waiting until they had shut—or rather, slammed the door, I crept up to the campervan and prayed it wasn't locked. It was.

So was the car. *Great.* Sitting on the steps was not an option unless I wanted to add the sound of my mother's sexual exploits to the list of things I needed therapy for, so I accepted my fate and returned to the party.

If I was going to be cold and lonely, I decided I would do it on a full stomach, so I piled snacks onto a plate, collected another burger, and found a new spot in the trees from which to watch my brother.

"There you are!" Freddie declared, walking towards me with a beer in hand. "I thought you weren't coming for a minute."

"That was my plan." I groaned.

"Do you want a drink?" Freddie asked, ignoring my tone entirely. I shook my head. "A dance?"

I laughed. "Definitely not."

"Why?"

A simple question with a million negative answers. "I just don't."

"You could come nearer the fire and meet my friends?"

Gazing into Freddie's eyes, my stomach fluttered. That smile was so bloody dangerous. I gulped. "Thanks, but I'll stay here."

Undeterred, Freddie sat next to me.

"What are you doing?"

"Sitting—obviously." Freddie grinned, making my stomach flip again. "If you won't come to me, I'll just have to come to you." He reached over, stole a crisp, and theatrically chewed on it.

"Thief!"

"Stop me." He laughed, taking another crisp.

A giggle bubbled out of me from nowhere. "Haven't you got better things to do than steal from me?"

"Nope." Freddie took a third crisp.

"You've a field full of people to entertain you—"

Freddie shrugged. "I want the one in the trees."

Suddenly all the sound around me faded to nothing. We stared at each other for what seemed like an eternity and my skin tingled in a way I hadn't felt before. Freddie hesitantly lifted his right hand, gently tucking a loose curl behind my ear. Frozen, I didn't move. Spellbound, I didn't want to.

Encouraged by my lack of retort or retreat, Freddie stroked the side of my cheek as he slowly leant in. Our eyes darted, trying to read whether the other was serious. My inner voice screamed with delight and fear simultaneously as our lips met. His eyes closed and mine followed. Somehow instinct took over. My arms wrapped around his neck while his hands slipped down my back, pulling me closer, kissing me deeper.

Footsteps behind me jolted my eyes open. Freddie felt my body tense and pulled back a little. As I looked at him, afraid he would regret his actions, he smiled—broadly.

"Freddie?" a voice called from somewhere near the fire. "*Freddie?*"

We both turned towards the party.

"You better see who needs you," I said, trying to catch my breath.

Freddie sighed as his name was called again. "Fine," he said, beginning to stand up, "but I'll be back." He paused, reached for my jawline once more, gently kissed my lips, and then sprung to his feet.

As Freddie was greeted by his friends, I rubbed my fingertips over my lips, too surprised to know how I felt about this unexpected development. A noise from behind me turned my head. I had forgotten hearing anyone moments earlier. When I realised it was Mrs Boxton from number seven, my eyes rolled. She was the park's nosey neighbour—of course *she* witnessed my first kiss.

"What the fuck is she doing here?" Kimberley Jenkins' slurred voice shouted. "Don't tell me that fucking feral Jailbird lives here? Freddie, honey, she's a psycho!"

Suddenly all eyes bore into me. I felt like their stares were chasing the ghost of my hope into the fire. That tiny slither of teenage normality was all I was allowed before I had to be dragged kicking and screaming back into my reality. Weeks ago, Freddie had been right. The shadows were the only place I relaxed at all, but now even that was being ripped from me. Slowly Freddie had crept into my shadows. I doubted him. He doubted himself. For a second we had both forgotten ourselves and it was almost beautiful, but now he was being reminded of the folly of choosing me in any way, shape, or form.

Possibly alcohol had altered his inhibitions. Freddie didn't look or behave drunk though. Kimberley was drunk—or at least well on the way to being so. Her inhibitions were decidedly lax. If they weren't, she would not have screamed her disgust at me. Our disdainful truce involved hate filled silence, not public humiliation.

Why could I not have anything? Not one friend—one kiss—without everything crashing down?

"Freddie!" Kimberley grabbed his arm when he didn't reply. "Answer me, Freddie!"

Kimberley's sister stepped forward. "What's wrong?"

"I think Freddie was just talking to that crazy bitch!" Kimberley responded angrily. "If you're dating him, Kaz, you need to control what he talks to better."

"What's wrong with her?" Kaz asked, staring at me as though I were a rabid dog, not a person. "Freddie, do you know her?"

All eyes, including mine, waited for Freddie to speak. He opened his mouth but hesitated. I knew what was running through his head. Commit social suicide and admit you just kissed a girl that your girlfriend's sister says is psychotic, or lie, and say I'm just a girl who lives on site who he barely knows.

In that moment, I was filled with disgust, but not for Freddie. For me. I had left a crack in my door and allowed him to stick his toe in. You raised every hair on my body and without making a conscious decision, I stood up. I wondered if You might attack and defend my honour—or settle the score that Kimberley seemed to be eternally raising. You was certainly angry enough, I could feel them all around me, but as quickly as my fist was clenched by a force beyond me, it released.

You gave me a second to decide.

Ceremoniously flicking my fingers as if their presence made me dirty, I spun on my heels and calmly walked into the woods. Kimberley and her friends' voices grumbled and jeered behind me but I did not take them in. I refused to.

As the darkness of the woods claimed me, my eyes caught the glare of blue, swirling lights ahead. My ears rang, but through the noise I heard *run* whispered by my only true friend. My legs answered You's command.

Leaves and twigs crunched under my feet and, like a moth to a flame, I charged towards the blue lights knowing they were signalling disaster. An ambulance was outside our caravan and two figures emerged pushing a person on a stretcher with a fourth person—Mr Forde—anxiously pacing behind. His eyes landed on me as I sped towards them.

"Cassie, oh, Cassie," Mr Forde spluttered.

"What happened?" I asked, staring at my barely conscious mother.

The paramedics looked at me with forlorn, patient eyes. "Do you know—"

"She's my mum!" I grasped the edge of the stretcher. "Mum? Are you okay? Mum?" Seeing her twisted, unresponsive face, my voice grew tighter, more desperate, with every syllable.

"Your mum has had a stroke, sweetie. We need to get her to hospital as fast as possible." The paramedic took my hand and spoke softly. "Time is essential right now. Do you understand?"

I did understand but nothing on this earth would make me ready for it.

"Do you want to ride with us?"

My brain clicked from slow motion to panic. "My brother. I need to fetch my brother. Can I—"

"Can you drive?" The paramedic said.

"Y—yes."

"Then get your brother and meet us at the hospital. I'm afraid we cannot wait."

Fred Forde stood with his hands round the back of his head with tears flowing down his face as Mum was packed into the ambulance.

"What happened?" I asked. He stared at me. I repeated my question, shaking his arm. His mouth flapped like a fish—not wholly unlike his son had when questioned by his friends about me only minutes earlier—but he said nothing. "Did you hurt her?" I screamed.

"No—no," he stuttered, "of course not. We were, well, you know, *having fun*... and then suddenly she—she *stopped*."

"Dad?" Freddie's voice echoed between the caravans as he ran across the drive towards us. "Did that ambulance just leave here? What happened?"

"Your dad fucked my mum and then she had a stroke." I watched my words bite into Freddie's face. Despite my anger and anguish, it pained me to speak so crudely to him, yet there was no time for pain—only action mattered. "I'm going to get Joey."

Striding past, Freddie's fingers grasped my arm. "Cassie, I—"

"*I'm going to get Joey*," I repeated, shaking my arm free.

"Do you need a ride?"

"No."

"Are you sure?" asked Old Fred, encouraged by his son's offer.

"Sure."

"We could—"

I stopped, glaring between father and son. "You've done enough, don't you think?"

Finding my brother, my heart sank at his happy, laughing face. Somehow it would have been easier to tell him if he was already sad, but instead I had to watch as my words turned his rosy cheeks white. There was no need to urge his compliance after that. His initial boyish, teasing expression flipped from *my sister isn't taking me home yet* to *why aren't we already in the car?*

Walking through the hospital corridors, my body felt numb. Only my left hand had any sensation as I desperately held onto my brother's sweaty fingers. We were shown to a waiting room and anxiously watched as doctors and nurses darted up and down the halls. It seemed like an eternity passed before anyone brought us news and when they did it was not the news either of us wanted to hear.

Words like subdural haematoma, seizure, and stroke were floated in front of me. It was a hideous game of charades and no one was winning. Internally I thanked the doctor for their patience as my mind struggled to organise the information being thrown at me. Nothing made sense. Then, as if plucked out of the air, one sentence clicked into place, causing a new flood of emotion to run through me.

"Excuse me," I said, raising my hand as though I were in school. "Did you just say that Mum has been seen for seizures *recently*?" The doctor looked at me quizzically. "As in, not just today?"

Reality bit.

The headaches were more than headaches and Mum knew it.

She knew it and said nothing. Even though saying nothing potentially meant leaving Joey and me totally unprepared.

"She knew this was coming?" Joey asked, sounding way more mature than he should have.

"Not exactly, no," the doctor replied carefully. "She was on medication hoping to prevent this. She has been having tests..."

My mind raced, suddenly translating odd comments and connecting the dots between times she was late collecting us, the phone calls she missed, and the hospital name tag on her wrist. Possibly she didn't want to admit the severity of the situation to herself, let alone us. I tried to defend her actions, telling myself it was impossible to say how I would behave were our roles reversed, but as I gazed at Joey, I became angry for attempting to lie for her. I knew instantly that I would do everything to protect my children from abandonment first and foremost.

"...the next twenty-four hours are critical." The end of the doctor's sentence brought me back into the present.

Joey didn't cry until the doctor left. Possibly I should not have let him hear the conversation, yet he deserved to know the truth. However, it wasn't until a social worker arrived that our new reality truly laid itself before me.

"I can take care of him," I said firmly.

The middle-aged lady hugged her folder to her chest and smiled sympathetically. "You're not eighteen, honey, I'm not legally allowed to—"

"I'm perfectly capable of—"

"I am not—"

"I can drive, I have money, I—"

"Have school," the social worker cut in.

"That's nothing new!" Desperation ran through me. I was so close but so far. Ten months too far in the eyes of the law.

"Joey, your next of kin is listed as your paternal aunt, er—" Ignoring me, the social worker's eyes darted over her paperwork. "Ah, yes, Trisha Thompson. Shall I call her?"

"There's no need." I replied.

"I'll just stay with my sister until Mum is better," Joey said sweetly.

The social worker sighed. "That could be a very long time." She looked me straight in the eyes. Her mouth said nothing, but her face said, *if ever.* She gazed again at Joey. "I know your sister wants to care for you, but I have to follow the law, and the law says she is not old enough to be your legal guardian. I am so sorry, but—"

The door swung open and Trisha walked in.

Fucking social worker. So much for *shall I call her?*

To be fair to Trisha, she refrained from any open disgust at my presence and spoke to Joey with true affection. She knew what was coming and out of loyalty to her deceased brother, she would take on his son without complaint. She would not, however, take me on. Part of her might have felt pity for me, but not enough to keep Joey and me together.

"She has an uncle," Trisha said matter-of-factly to the social worker. "Call him."

"I'll stay with my mother, thank you," I said curtly. "Can I see her now?" I was fed up with being spoken over and wanted to see Mum for myself.

The social worker puffed out her cheeks. "She is in surgery, honey, but—"

"Then I'll wait." I sat down and crossed my arms until Joey curled up next to me.

Putting my arm around him, we waited for hours. Trisha came in and out, leaving for the bathroom, a coffee, or to try and find out news before we did. If it wasn't for Joey and You's comforting arms, I think I would have chased her down the halls with a chair, but instead I ignored her cold blue eyes as they rested on me. It was a look that I would never reconcile with. The scowl, the set of the chin, the ice was too like her brother's. Joey's features were similar but had melted through my defences and reminded me of our unbreakable blood bond. Trisha neither wanted nor cared for such things. She had no need to. She only needed to love Joey—and that was easy. Thankfully, she did let Joey and me visit Mum alone though.

With her face twisted and head heavily bandaged, I almost didn't recognise Mum. The doctor had explained all of the above, telling us not to expect any response, but my mother's vacant, not quite unconscious expression cut into my soul. Trapped in a void within me, my tears would not flow—although Joey cried enough for the both of us.

Seeing Mum removed all hope of this being a blip in our childhood, and I immediately knew I would lose my brother that day. Trisha would raise him, and I would have to take a backseat. Joey would fight it for a moment, but ultimately he also knew that our lives had been irrevocably ripped apart.

There were no blips for me.

Ever.

Everything had to tear.

When Joey and I hurriedly left the caravan, along with her car keys, I had grabbed my mother's handbag. Sitting in the hospital, seeing her in such a state, it felt like a ridiculous thing to have done—she would not be buying a drink, putting on makeup, or calling anyone—yet after Joey left with Trisha, I clung to the ornate leather bag as though it were a person.

In my solitary state of bedside watcher, my brother's words rang in my ears. He was so young yet understood the implications of that day perfectly. As he bravely stood before me, he had made me promise to visit him often, call every day, and finish my studies.

"Do it for yourself first," he whispered into my stomach as we hugged, "but also for me. You and I are always yours. A bond that cannot be broken."

Out of the corner of my eye, I saw confusion strike across Trisha's face, but I smiled knowingly to Joey when he looked up at me. To anyone but me his grammar was off, but on the lonely days ahead, those words would comfort me.

While a doctor checked on Mum, I watched their face, waiting for a word, a smile—something resembling hope which I had otherwise lost. Deciding the doctor would make an excellent poker player, I cracked, asking, "What do you think?" They gazed straight into my eyes but said nothing. I was sure they were weighing up the most diplomatic, evasive answer they could muster. "Please, be honest," I begged. "Is there any chance that she could ever be the same?"

"I am so sorry, but if your mother survives this, she is going to require a lot of after care."

"How long for?" I asked, cautiously.

"Months—probably years." The doctor paused, chewing on their bottom lip.

"But you think she'll die, don't you?"

"It is too soon to say." The doctor bobbed their head. "But..." I stared at them, desperately hoping for a straight answer. "We'll see. Try to get some rest. Is there someone I can call? Grandparents? Friends?"

"My grandparents are dead." That was only mostly true. Dad's parents died when I was very little. Mum's parents moved to Spain when she was a teenager, then disowned her when she married. Her father died somewhere in between and her mum remarried. I don't remember ever meeting any of them.

"You will need someone to help you, even if you wish to care for yourself. I hear you have an uncle. Can I—"

"I'll do it. Thanks." I smiled, holding my calm expression. The doctor nodded again, got up, squeezed my shoulder, and left.

New Year is supposed to be a good thing. The turning of a new, potentially exciting chapter in your life. All excitement, all hope or ambition, had been stripped from me. The thought that an existence as my mother's carer was my best-case scenario churned my insides. Had she been blameless, had this been a mere accident to mark what was otherwise a love-filled life, I might not have felt the anger that I felt in that moment. But I had the aching feeling that these seizures directly came from Hal's attack. She knew she was sick but left neither guardian nor guide for me. Sure, she left instructions—albeit minimal ones—in her file for Trisha to be called to help Joey, but for me she left nothing but a burden.

My chest tightened, and I couldn't breathe.

I was trapped.

She had trapped me all over again.

Feeling my increasing distress, You rattled in and around me. It was as though a gale had brewed inside the hospital ward—and You was the storm and I the eye.

My heart raced.

My head spun.

Then darkness hit.

EVERYTHING CHANGES

The gentle call of a nurse woke me from my slumber. She stroked my back with tenderness, but as my consciousness returned, I jolted away from her touch like a rabbit in the jaws of a fox. Startled, the nurse gazed at me apologetically.

"I'm so sorry," she said after composing herself. "I didn't mean to give you an extra shock."

Rubbing my weary eyes, her choice of words seemed strange. "Extra?"

Her eyes drifted to my mother's bed. The room was silent. No beeping monitors counting her heart. No heart beats. No breaths. No pulse. Only the cold reality of death.

There was my mother. Her face frozen in eternal rest as it laid on the pristine pillow. Her arms laid neatly by her sides. I stared at her. But she would never again stare back.

My throat caved in on itself, forming a lump the size of a brick. The nurse seemed to be waiting for me to say something, yet I had nothing to say. No lament to wail, no hate to spout. Numbness overcame me, and I became it.

All of my plans of escaping her, the town, the life she was forming for me—or rather around me—all crashed down in that moment. My focus of becoming self-sufficient so I could fully take care of Joey was all for nought. Yet he had survived our combined childhood of trauma. I had protected him as best I could. Now, Trisha would set him up within her family, and I would watch from the sidelines.

Slowly, I sat on the side of Mum's bed, afraid that if I took my eyes off her, I would forget her face. But that wasn't her true face. Her beautiful, symmetrical face. The stroke had robbed her of that.

"I'm so sorry," the nurse repeated. I had almost forgotten that she was there.

Still clutching Mum's bag, I nodded as my mind danced from one thought to another. What was I going to do next? The social worker would surely be on my back again now. There was only one person I really knew to call, but I didn't have his number.

"The doctor will come and sign her death certificate. Can I—"

"Would it be ok if I had some time alone with her?" I asked, cutting the nurse off.

"Of course, of course," she replied, instantly leaving the room. "I will be back in a while."

"Thank you." Watching her shut the door, I smiled, then turned back to the bag on my lap. Pulling out Mum's mobile phone, I felt weird. It had been years since I tried cracking into her phone, but now I was beyond avoiding the tales of a teacher or satisfying childish whim. I needed her fingerprint to unlock the screen and time for that was fast running out. Taking Mum's cold hand, I pressed her finger on the sensor. It was a practical, relatively innocent act, but my skin shuddered as though I were a dirty spy. Vowing to make my efforts count, I quickly changed the settings, removing the security requirement, and then opened up Mum's contact list.

Taking one last look at my mother before the noise of the world returned, I wished that I had words to say to her. I wished it was only love that I felt. It was there, along with heartache and gut-wrenching bereavement, but other, darker, feelings mixed and stifled the more natural display that others expected to see.

Kimberley's words echoed in my ears. *She's a feral Jailbird...a psycho.*

Suddenly a warmth surrounded me. There was no need to turn around, I knew it was You. My comforter and protector. In my heart, I also knew what You had done. They had ensured my release from a life of shackles.

Now I just needed to know where my newfound freedom would take me.

As the mobile screen was about to turn off, I hit the call button and waited.

"Michelle?" Uncle Gary's surprised voice came out of the phone.

"It's not Michelle," I said numbly.

"*Cassie?*"

"Yeah."

Gary exhaled deeply. "Wow, it's so good to hear from you. Are you okay?"

"Not really. I need your help."

My uncle still looked the same except his wavy brown hair had streaks of grey and his eyes now crinkled in the corners when he smiled. He didn't smile when he gazed past me to my mother. Instead he stood, holding the frame at the end of her bed, silently weeping.

It struck me as an odd reaction for an estranged woman who he had fought with as much as anything since my father's imprisonment. They got on, then they didn't. They swore, laughed, then swore again. The last time Mum had mentioned him, she had told me about Gary's basement full of drugs. For her, it was fine to profit from the sale of drugs, but she would not live on the production site. Don't shit where you eat—or something like that. Possibly it was one of the most sensible things she had decided on because if the police did raid the place, living on top of a drug factory was pretty darn obvious. Yet here I was, openly inviting Gary back into my life because she had not provided me with any other alternatives.

Gary willingly signed whatever paperwork was pushed in front of him, turning himself into my official guardian. Years ago I wanted that. I wanted to live in his annex. Now I wasn't sure, although the offer was renewed—or possibly more accurately, simply assumed.

"I need to sort things out at the caravan site," I said as we sat opposite one another in the hospital cafeteria. It seemed like I had lived there for weeks, not two days, and the prospect of walking into the daylight was just too much.

"I can come with you. We don't have to pack everything in one day if you don't want to. I'm sure I can arrange with this Fred Forde guy to let you keep the rent until you're sorted."

I scoffed. "Old Fred will be okay." Gary raised a questioning eyebrow at me as he drank his coffee. "They never said anything, but it seems that he was kind of seeing Mum. They were *at it* when she had her stroke—so the least he can do is not kick me out."

Gary nearly spat his drink at me but thankfully kept his lips closed long enough to swallow. At first, I thought he looked angry but his expression mellowed as his mind ran through whatever thoughts he wasn't sharing. "I'm sorry," he said eventually, gazing at me with sad eyes. "I should have stuck around regardless of—" He sighed deeply, staring up at the ceiling.

"Regardless of what?" I asked.

Gary's body deflated. "*Of everything.*"

———

Driving to the caravan, Joey's tears and my uncle's words weighed heavily on me. I wasn't sorry that I had been the one to tell Joey though. It had to be me as much as I had to see him in his new home—even if it would be one of only a handful of times that I ever set foot on Trisha's doorstep. In the future it would be: collect Joey from school, take him to the cinema, watch him at pony club, or feed him tonight.

This new year was truly a rebirth—although someone forgot to tell my racing mind and exhausted body. Gary's *everything* felt more and more relevant, but I feared there was a point, a specific point, somewhere in the middle of that *everything* that one day I would take issue with. I needed Uncle Gary to just be my uncle, not the keeper of secrets, but You whispered warnings in my ear as I parked beside the campervan.

Both campervan and caravan were in darkness, but a half-moon combined with reflections from the neighbours' properties to illuminate my way—or would have done if I wasn't so reluctant to open the front door. Trisha had already taken most of Joey's things, but Mum's room was untouched. The bedsheets were still knotted where she and Old Fred had been, marking the last few carefree moments of her life. An ironic chuckle burst out of me. It was consensual, so maybe it wasn't the worst way to go.

As though I were a robot, I began packing but quickly ran out of bags. Slumping on the bed, I decided I was doing this all wrong. Parked next to me was a home on wheels. It was plenty big enough for You and me but small enough that I could drive it on my licence. Collecting my things, I carted everything I cared for into the campervan. It didn't take long.

Returning from the campervan, my stomach flipped as Freddie sat on the porch with his legs dangling over the edge. Having begged Gary to allow me to pack alone, I begged him again to let me speak to Old Fred Forde, but I had forgotten to think of Freddie. Seeing him, I wanted to feel anger towards him for his cowardice but something stopped me.

Maybe I was simply too tired.

When he walked towards me with his face furrowed, I just said, "She's gone."

"Joey told me," he said gently, "I'm so sorry. I went to the hospital but your aunt told me to go. I came again, but then you were gone."

"She's not my aunt."

"Right." Freddie ruffled his hair anxiously. "Look—" He stepped towards me. "About the other night... before, before—"

Irritation and disappointment hit me. "Forget it." Shaking my head, I strode towards him, accidentally brushing my sleeve against his jacket as I passed by.

"I can't—I don't want to forget it."

Bitterness rose within me. "Which part? The kiss, your girlfriend, or your father with my mother?"

Freddie grimaced.

"It's not exactly an evening I will forget, I suppose," I muttered, opening the door. "Did you know our parents were at it?"

"No. I thought he liked her, but no, I didn't."

"Too busy with your own games."

"I'm *not* with Kaz."

I could feel You rushing around me. "That's not what I saw."

"What she wants and what I want are not the same thing, Cassie. And just because she and her sister spout shit doesn't make any of it true." Uninvited, he followed me inside, leaning on the wall separating the living room and kitchen. Trying to ignore him, I pulled a carton of orange juice from the fridge and filled a glass. "I'm sorry I didn't defend you immediately. I was surprised. I froze. I shouldn't have." He paused, and I scoffed. "For what it is worth, I did when you left—before I came after you. You're *not* a psycho—or a Jailbird."

"Maybe I am." I said, raising my glass before taking a sip of juice.

"*No*, you're not."

Freddie stared at me earnestly. He seemed to believe his words; the trouble was I was beginning to believe mine.

"I'm not staying here much longer. Can you tell your dad?"

"Where are you going?" Freddie stepped towards me.

"I'm not sure yet." I shrugged. "My uncle has offered his place."

"You could stay."

"Not in here. I don't want to. Not now. I am going to empty this place, then I'll decide."

Freddie glanced around the room. "Shall I help?"

Together we packed the remains of Joey's things, the kitchen, and living room into boxes. For years Mum had kept our earthly belongings to a minimum. I guess she was always reluctant to take on things that she would have to leave behind in a hurry. Possibly the fight had been knocked out of her too many times so a hasty flight was just better. Only then did it truly occur to me that she was probably seeking love all of her life, only she never found a healthy way of giving or receiving it. Sneaking glances at Freddie, I wondered if I was doomed to follow in her footsteps.

Gary called wanting to take me to the funeral directors. Booking the basics over the phone, I agreed to go with him to finalise everything in two days. Unable to cope with ringing all of Mum's friends, I selected 'text all' on her phone and wrote:

Dear Friends of Michelle Thompson,
I regret to inform you of my mother's passing following a stroke.
If you would like to pay your respects and come to her funeral it
will be at the below location, date, and time.
Yours,
Cassie Reilly

It felt cold, but it was all I could do. When Mum's phone immediately lit up with call upon call, Freddie listened to me repeat the story again and again until my lips trembled. Gently taking the phone from my hand, he turned it off and pulled me into a hug. Then, for the first time, I cried.

The neighbour's curtains twitched each time I opened the door, but only George, the gardener, spoke to me. I was as grateful for his few words of kindness as I was the others' silence. Joey was the sweet bubbly boy who had won them over. Without him, I was the weird girl who prowled in the woods. They undoubtedly saw my things hanging in the campervan window and wondered how long it would be until I left. When I stood on the sidestep, swinging Gordon's bat, they probably prayed it would be sooner than later.

Why that stupid bat comforted me, I couldn't say. Sense would have compelled me to buy a new one—one unsullied by its previous owner or acts of violence. Perhaps it was the most tangible form of You's protection I had—and as my mind couldn't forget why I had needed protection, I also couldn't replace the symbol of my protector.

Moving the bat into the campervan was my penultimate act before locking up the caravan and handing over the keys. It was my signal that that was where I would now sleep. I couldn't say *find rest* because rest had become a unicorn to me.

Sorting Mum's clothes, books, and makeup had been relatively easy to deal with, but her drawer of photos, trinkets, and papers made me choke. Seeing her handwriting, her few notes, even on the most boring subjects challenged my frozen senses—so I left them to last.

"Your mum has a jewellery box here," Freddie said, pulling out a maroon-coloured box from the back of her bedside cabinet.

"Oh?" I said, flicking through the few old family photos that hadn't perished in our house fire years ago. "That's not a jewellery box. See, I have it here." I lifted a mahogany box off Mum's dressing table.

"Huh, maybe not. I guess it's more of a fancy filing cabinet—do you know where the key is?"

It took us thirty minutes to realise the key had been taped to the base of the box. Obviously, we did not have careers as thieves ahead of us. Not that the contents of the box were really worth stealing.

Our passports, school letters, early childhood drawings, doctor's reports detailing her secret treatment, her divorce papers, Darren's death certificate, bank and insurance details, and a PO Box receipt were the sum total of her hidden treasure.

"Well, that was anticlimactic," Freddie groaned.

"Yeah," I replied, running my fingers over the only drawing that wasn't solely Joey's. I say *solely* because at some point Joey had added himself and a swirling shadow in the tree that stood beside me. It was unusual for me to draw myself, but there I was, kneeling on the ground with my arms outstretched and face uncharacteristically smiling. It was my idea of happiness because the earth in front of me was planted with saplings poking through—beautiful plants that thrived thanks to the rays coming from the bright sun above.

More than anything, I missed the sun. Now I had neither earth nor sun.

Somehow, I would have to make my own.

Freddie's stomach growled, pulling me out of my thoughts.

I chuckled. "You sound like you're starving."

He laughed. "That was *your* stomach."

"Really?"

"Yes, really." He took my hand. "Come on, let's get dinner."

———

As promised, Gary was waiting for me outside the funeral directors. He was wearing smart black trousers and a tie with a white shirt, and I wondered if he thought we were burying Mum there and then instead of arranging it. On the actual day I would wear my mother's long, black dress and favourite formal jacket—my last act of appeasing her fashion tastes—but that day I wore black jeans, an orange and black striped woollen jumper, and matching scarf.

Gary did most of the talking but asked my opinion on everything—except how I was planning to pay. When the funeral director quietly mentioned payment, I went to fumble for my purse, hoping my meagre savings would be enough, but Gary pushed a card across the table and said, "Bill all to here," before I could utter a word.

The idea of owing him anything made me anxious, so as soon as we were outside, I said, "I will pay you back." I spoke in earnest, even though I had no idea how or when I would manage it.

"You will not." Gary held me by the elbows. Instinct made me want to recoil, but he spoke so softly that I forced myself to keep still. "Cassie, it is I who owes you."

My face screwed up in my confusion. "How?"

"Will you come to mine now?"

I paused, asking myself if I was ready for that. Everything had already changed, so why not just go with it? Mum might have hated Gary's home, but it was the family business...

Sensing my reluctance, Gary shrugged. "Our restaurant is three streets away. Why not sit and talk things over properly?"

"*Our what?*"

It was Gary's turn to screw up his face, but he quickly replaced the frown with a beaming smile. "Come."

***

Following Gary's car, I passed by Dee's house for the first time since leaving—since the day that marked the beginning of Mum's end. Hal's attack had effectively killed her. No part of me doubted it, even if I couldn't prove it.

You should have killed him, I said to myself with passion.

My anger had not passed, but gauging by the boarded-up windows, the moment had. That didn't stop me whispering an appeal for karma to catch him though.

Ignoring the large front carpark, Gary's truck slowly curled behind a restaurant so I guided Mum's car—now mine—through the narrow archway and parked next to him. Getting out, I looked at the building. It wasn't just a restaurant, it was a nightclub. Somewhere the likes of Kaz or Kimberley Jenkins might frequent but not me.

Gary jolted his head towards the entrance, and I followed. As we approached, a security guard smiled and held the door open, "Afternoon, sir, madam," he said.

"Thank you," I whispered.

"Cheers, Marcus," Gary said. "Is it busy today?"

"Yes, sir, very."

"Excellent."

The inviting smell of fresh food and wine hit me as I entered the darkened hallway. Gary led us away from the music and sound of happy, dining customers into a private room. It was the kind of room you'd expect to see in gangster movies with low, intimate lighting and a large table for entertaining a select few. That day You and I were the few.

"What is this place?" I asked.

"Your legacy, my dear."

A grin spread over my uncle's face, and I suddenly realised I didn't know him at all. I wasn't sure if I liked it, but I was certain that You did not. Silently I begged them to hear Gary out as I felt my skin prickle in electric anticipation.

"This place is Dad's?"

"This place is *yours*—if you want it."

"How so?"

"Your father left me as custodian of your assets until you are twenty-one. Some you will receive at eighteen, but some of it requires you to be a little older."

"And what exactly are my assets?"

"This nightclub and restaurant, three other restaurants, the funeral directors, and approximately fifty housing projects—both in construction and rental."

"I thought you had a drug business?"

Gary chuckled. "I prefer the term *empire*, but yes, that enterprise has allowed for all others to flourish."

"Or the others flourish to hide the enterprise," I said dryly.

"Precisely." Gary seemed impressed. "Cassie, will you finally take your place in the family and join me? Say you'll be my apprentice."

The words were those from a play—exactly what I wanted to hear but answered next to nothing. "Why are you only now telling me this? Why have I been living like a rat in cupboards when this is supposedly mine?"

"Your mother wanted her independence. She preferred to sever ties and live an alternative life." Gary spoke so calmly, so matter-of-factly, for a moment I believed him, but You nipped at my skin.

Something didn't add up.

"She took payments though."

"She did, of course," Gary nodded. "For child support."

I felt like a fly hovering in front of a web filled with treats. It looked inviting, it looked like a welcoming place to rest, but my heart told me there was a spider waiting to catch me out.

"Why did you leave me for years? Why not actually be there for me?"

"Your mother forbade it."

"But you were around when I was younger. You had the money—you *have* the money!" My face stung with betrayal. "You left me to the whims of drunks, rapists, and narcissists! You could have fucking stepped in at any point and insisted—"

"To what?" Ashen, Gary slowly approached and stood before me. "What happened to you?"

He meant *you* as in *me*, but *you* as in *You* rallied around me. I hadn't planned to, but it was the first time I had vocalised my abusive past. The guilt it struck across Gary's face made me wish I hadn't. I didn't want his guilt, nor his misplaced pity. He had the power to step in years ago and chose not to. Now, You wasn't going to let anyone touch me without permission again.

"Don't fucking touch me," I spat, feeling You's phantom fingers help me take a step back. "I don't need your pity. Tell me about my inheritance or let me leave." My face set like stone with my chin raised high. The mafia child would be reborn. Even if he would not see me, I would take the place my father left me and hope to make my own sun—or burn it all trying.

HOMECOMING

After the funeral, returning to the caravan park no longer felt like my best option. I couldn't call it home anymore—I never really could, but once the caravan was empty of all signs of me ever having lived there, it definitely wasn't. Old Fred stuttered and blushed as he opened his front door the morning I handed him the keys. Part of me considered continuing to clean for him in the hope that a humble existence might reveal the reason my mother chose to live as we did when riches were literally at the other end of a phone call, but I felt destiny calling.

"There's no time limit on you leaving. You're welcome back any time. You can park your van by the shower block," Old Fred said. Behind his smile I saw him lamenting his words, but guilt was working in my favour so I thanked him and went on my way. Who knows whether he and Mum would really have lasted or if his affections went beyond amused attraction, but there was nothing like an untimely death to make memory softer or hearts fonder.

"Do you want me to drive the campervan and you take your car?" Freddie asked after I explained that I was planning to move to Gary's driveway. "You can give me a ride home though, right?"

"Sure, that would be great. Thank you," I replied.

Seeing all my worldly belongings drive in front of me felt weird and unsettling, but I found that less unnerving than Freddie's grin as he got out of the driver's seat. He'd been kind and supportive since Mum's death but largely serious. The cheeky grin had been measured, like he didn't dare push me. That friendship was the closest to comfortable I had ever felt, but now he was slowly returning to his cocky, playful self. The self that had breached my defences and kissed me on New Year's Eve.

It made me nervous.

———

Sometimes, I would park my car out of sight and walk with You through the woods to visit my wild garden after school. It was the only way I could detox from a difficult day. Each day I thought about dropping out, but I always turned up anyway. Gary seemed to approve of my choices although I couldn't decide if that was a good reason to continue or quit. Every day he would cook me dinner and ask me to move out of the van and into his annex. Sense said it was the obvious, practical choice, however, I ate his food, listened to his chatter, and returned to my van on the driveway.

"When I'm eighteen, will you be demoted?" I asked cautiously one night.

Gary's face fell but he quickly laughed. "When you're eighteen, Cassie, I will sign over your trust fund, but I will still run everything. It will take you years to thoroughly understand the logistics of this business. It is a family enterprise. We will both have our roles."

"But you'll start teaching me properly?"

"Absolutely."

"Then I will live with you properly."

Gary beamed—I mean truly beamed. You still raced around me, speeding my heart as they crackled through the air, but there was no denying that Gary was happy about my announcement.

He was true to his word and presented me to every employee who didn't already know who I was. Some I recognised from years ago. It surprised me how my childish mind had held onto their names and faces. Possibly my presence surprised them too. A few I distinctly remembered asking my father to remove me from discussions and them being told I was the future of the company. I never asked, but I wondered if they remembered.

Touring the basement of Gary's house, it was impossible not to think of my mother. She had every right to hate the idea of living there. The whole building was a massive headline in the making. Sure, it had been designed to be off grid, but Gary's pride had clouded his judgement. It wasn't my place to question though. I was there to learn. Maybe to balance. Gary labelled me as the future generation, but in truth I was still deciding if I truly belonged in their world. The only world I knew as mine was amongst the trees far from any crowd, drug factory, housing operation, or whatever business you cared to mention.

The greenhouse appealed. In there I could get my hands dirty with pleasure, but the crops were not my own. The apprentice does not choose. They follow. They wait.

"We need to discuss what to do with your old house," Gary said one morning sitting at his breakfast bar buttering toast.

"Excuse me?" I sipped my tea, half burning my tongue. "What house?"

"The Old School."

My eyes bulged. "Dad's house?"

"Yeah."

You twitched at the mention of our old home. "It burnt down, remember?"

"Of course, but what do you want to do with the site now? Sell?"

My neck arched forward—almost on its own. "Am I missing something?" I narrowed my eyes, staring at my uncle. "Didn't Mum sell it?"

"It was never hers to sell. Didn't she tell you?"

Biting back a sarcastic response, I said, "No, she didn't."

"Figures."

"So it's still Dad's?"

"He put the house, the garden, and the woods behind it in your name, Cassie." Gary chortled. "And a field beyond that, which really pissed off another developer." He laughed louder. "I've acquired a few of the houses on the street in recent years too, so it's a huge plot that you now own."

"Have you done anything to it?"

"We cleared the burnt house, that's all."

"What about the shed?"

"It'll be wild with vines, but still there—much to your mother's displeasure, no doubt." He paused, smiling. "You loved that shed."

I grinned. "Yes, indeed."

After school, I drove to my old house for the first time in years. The hairs on my skin stood to attention as I pulled up onto the empty driveway and tears rose as I viewed the spot where my house once stood. If my brain selected the right era, it was a happy home. A home of completion. My father was no saint, but he loved me. He centred my mother and held the family together.

Inevitably my mind slipped into latter years. Lonelier years. Violent years where I met my friend. Together we walked over the house and into the garden. It was entirely feral yet some of the plants I once tended to remained amongst the volunteer weeds.

I tutted to myself as I thought the word.

Weeds are simply defined by a plant growing in the wrong place.

Was that not what I had been for much of my life?

These plants were not unwanted by nature any more than I was unwanted by You. Nature claimed us as part of its wilderness, and I followed its call to the bottom of the garden and found my shed. The brambles had embraced it more than ever, just as they had my heart.

You spirited away through the cracks of the door frame, playing memories of old—both good and bad—from our time together there.

"No," I said out loud to any creature who cared to listen, "I will not sell your home."

Our home, whispered You.

"Our home," I repeated.

LETTERS FROM HEAVEN

Sheltering from the heat in a tree, my daydreams were interrupted by a rabbit darting past. Listening carefully, I heard light footsteps seconds before I saw a familiar figure.

"So you *do* still come here," Freddie's voice drifted through the woods.

"It seems so," I replied, returning his smile.

"I'd have met you earlier if you'd said."

My heart replied, *I would have, if I wasn't afraid to*. Instead, my head said, "Sorry."

"May I?" Freddie pointed to the spot next to me.

"Be my guest." A nervous giggle wriggled out of me. Since I moved we had texted more than seen each other. Honestly, I missed him, but I told myself it was for the best. I didn't completely believe it, but I told myself it anyway.

Freddie sat on the low-hanging branch next to me so closely our legs touched. "You always were happier in the trees."

I rolled my eyes. "I know. I'm weird."

"You're my kind of weird."

My eyes shot to his and were greeted by the grin that melted me. Warning bells rang in my ears. *No future, no future,* they screamed. While my heart soaked in the warmth of his gorgeous dark eyes, it fought with the alarms ringing in my head. *Why does everything have to have a future? Has ours not been upended already?*

As I questioned whether I was going mad, Freddie leant in, slowly wrapping his arm around me. Part of me—by then I had lost track of which part—likened his moves to a hunter creeping up on a deer, but if he was hunting me, he did it so tenderly that I did not want to take flight.

When our foreheads met, I sucked in my bottom lip. Air suddenly seemed to be in short supply as though the trees had forgotten to swap carbon dioxide for oxygen. Freddie took his time, giving me every opportunity to back away, but finally, after months of patience, his lips found mine again.

He started sweetly, continuously testing to see if I would object. I didn't. His embrace tightened, grew more passionate, and his hands wandered across my back, through my hair, and around my waist. The branch wasn't high, but we wobbled on it and pulled apart to check our balance. We laughed and Freddie slid out of the tree, holding out his hands. Without thought, I released myself into his arms and instantly he resumed our embrace.

He kissed my neck, sending shivers everywhere and weakening my knees. My arms crossed over his shoulders, allowing his hands to run under my shirt and upwards as I nibbled on his ear. We tumbled against the tree trunk, our kisses growing deeper and deeper, and I felt him growing harder and harder against my thigh.

My hands began unbuttoning his shirt and he hungrily did the same. In an instant, we were both topless and my nipples were being tasted one at a time as we sank to the ground. He rolled me on my back, kissing my lips, whilst slowly grinding himself against me before his hand expertly popped open the button on my shorts and slipped inside. My eyes sprung open. I wanted him to touch me and feared it all at once. Feeling trapped, my cruel mind's eye suddenly swapped Freddie's face for Gordon's and panic grasped every fibre of my being.

Scrabbling in the dirt, I cried out. Shocked, Freddie immediately backed away, allowing me to clamber to my feet whilst automatically reaching for a fallen branch. Confusion flashed across Freddie's face, and I felt sick.

Dropping the half rotten wood, I grabbed my top, shoved my bra into my pocket, and ran.

Sitting in my car, with tears streaming down my face, I felt defective. My hands were shaking too much to drive so I silently thanked Freddie for not chasing after me. I scoffed at myself. Why would he? He'd never want me now. There was an enormous difference between *kinda quirky and cute* and *just plain damaged*. There was no prize for guessing which I was.

Bursting into tears again, I slammed my hands on the dashboard, causing a pocket to pop up in front of the wheel. I stared at it as though an alien had landed. Until then, I didn't even know there was a compartment there. *Every day's a school day, huh?* I said to no one.

Wiping my steamed-up glasses on my shirt, I leant forward, peering into the compartment to see what was there. Part of me was hoping for a Narnia moment—it would have been bloody awkward accessing another world through that gap but I was desperate enough to try—but instead I found something that would, once deciphered, both lodge my thoughts on the earth *and* encourage me to reach for the sun.

Three bags of mints revealed themselves first, and I chuckled ironically. My mother having a sugar stash was not a great surprise. Occasionally, I found wrappers that she told me were Joey's and then told Joey were mine. I was an honest snacker and Joey liked to gloat, so we both knew she was lying, but sadly it took six months after her death to find the source of her lies. Continuing in the pocket, I found the logbook for the car—which would be handy when I eventually sold it but in the meantime would stop Gary pestering me for its service history—but it was the red file behind it which spiked my curiosity.

"*What the fuck?*" I said to my mother. Obviously, I didn't expect an answer, but why she had a letter from the post office reminding her to collect her PO Box mail, I didn't understand. Our mail had always been delivered to the caravan site. By that point, I had registered myself as resident at Gary's address and Fred had forwarded any junk or wayward mail. All insurance, all schooling, everything important, was redirected.

Pulling out my phone, I checked the time. Groaning, I accepted it was too late. The office would be closed, so I had a night to sweat out what Mum was up to. My mind skipped through the documents I had found after her death. The box. The maroon box. Didn't that have a PO Box receipt in it? Being old and dated between long-past house moves, I ignored it, thinking it was irrelevant.

My hands still shook, but I turned the key in the ignition and slowly drove home. The numerous solar panels gleamed in the evening sunshine, welcoming me back, but no one else was there, not even Gary's workers. They would come in soon for their nightshift. Fumbling with the keys, I opened the campervan door. It needed oiling so it creaked like an old floorboard, making me tiptoe. I mocked myself. Why was I creeping around in my own campervan?

Mum's maroon box was in the cupboard where I had left it. It had been so long since I had needed it, I had not bothered to carry it into the annex. Unsticking the key from the base, I released the lock, trying to discard thoughts of Freddie as I recalled him being with me when I found it the first time.

Eagerly removing the receipt from its envelope, my eyes scanned the paper, resting on a code at the bottom. It was a membership card of sorts. Slipping it into my bag, I locked up the campervan and went straight into the annex, hoping I would sleep because tomorrow I was determined to find out what I had just gained entry to.

Standing in front of the secured post box, I began to doubt whether I wanted to know what was in it. If there were hospital letters that spelt out what had already passed, demands for money, or information on old boyfriends I really didn't want to know. The answer was the other side of the door, yet my mind seemed to enjoy listing every possible option rather than simply seeking the truth. I felt You's impatience buzzing beside me. They too wanted to know.

"Okay," I whispered, reaching for the door, *"but don't blame me if you have to pick up the pieces again."*

As the door swung open, a noise must have escaped from me because a short, elderly lady in a light blue summer dress approached and peered up at me. "Are you alright, dear? Can I help you?"

Blinking, I tried to respond, but instead I pointed.

"Oh my, that is a lot of mail!" she said, staring at the mound of letters. "Do you have a bag?" I shook my head. "Here," she said, pulling a tote bag from her handbag, "have mine."

"Thank you," I said, turning over the dark brown bag with donkeys and carrots sprouting in various places. "Can I pay you for this?"

"Only with a smile." She beamed. "There! What greater reward is there?"

I thanked her again but she was already heading out of the door. With such a dysfunctional family, I never knew the joy of grandparents or truly experienced the blessing of spending time with the elderly. Missing out on stable parents had always bothered me more, but that brief encounter stirred a new longing as well as fulfilled a practical need.

You nudged my right hand, and I got the message—*fill the bag!*

Refusing to read any of them yet, I neatly placed each letter inside the tote bag, making use of every last bit of space. There were a few marketing flyers which I popped into the recycling bin in the corner of the room, but when I reached the bottom of the box, I also found a little parcel. The seal was unbroken and the postal mark was ten years old, but what struck me the most was the handwriting. It was Mum's.

"Did she send this to herself?" I muttered to You.

"Excuse me," I said to the member of staff, handing them Mum's membership letter. "How long is my PO Box rented for?"

The young girl tapped on her computer. "Huh," she said.

"Is everything okay?" I asked, fearing I had opened a can of worms.

"Yes, madam, perfectly okay. Sorry, I just don't see many non-business lifetime policies."

"Is there a reoccurring payment? I may need to change account if—"

"No, no. It was fully paid for in cash ten years ago. A Mrs Michelle Thompson and Miss Cassandra Reilly are named on the account and have a one-hundred-year lifetime membership." My mouth gaped as she spoke. "Is there a problem I can help you with?"

"No, no, thank you. I just wanted to be sure. I didn't know Mum hadn't emptied it, so I wanted to be sure any post wasn't lost."

The girl smiled sweetly. "Nope, it's all good in there. No one touches other people's letters."

"Wonderful. Thank you."

"Have a nice day!" She turned to the next customer, and I walked to the car. With each step my legs grew weaker and only the invisible assistance of You got me into the privacy of my own vehicle before I howled like a baby.

———

My Dearest Cassie,

How I miss you. Who knows if you ever read these letters or if you even want me to write them, but unless you, yourself, face me and tell me to stop, I will continue in the hope that we are not lost to one another. Do not worry for me though, I knew what prison would be. I knew what I had to do, what I had to be, and regret nothing except our separation. How are you? What are you doing now? Do you still sing to plants and get angry when they do not grow? Probably not, but I still hear your sweet voice and its melody lulls me to sleep each night.

You know where I am, should you want me.

Yours always,

Dad xx

All of the letters were redirected from my various old addresses to that post box. All originated from prison. All of them made me cry.

They varied in length over the years. I guess there are only so many ways to say, *I love you, I miss you, where are you?* Hatred for my mother hit an all-time high. Hatred and complete confusion. Why had she repeatedly told me my father refused to see me?

Why did she and Gary maintain the same lie?

My first thought was to drive to Gary and demand answers. I could hear You suggesting the use of Gordon's bat. But that was our combined pain. If I wanted the truth, I needed to be wiser.

More measured.

Less impulsive.

BEHIND BARS

Sitting in the visitors room, I trembled. The idea that this was an elaborate, cruel joke had kept me up all night and if it weren't for the clever use of subtle makeup, I would have looked terrible. I had Dee to thank for that, I suppose. Mum had moaned that I let Dee help when I would not entertain her efforts, but by then I was older, didn't live with a pervert, and Dee expertly used makeup without making it obvious. Nothing would compel me to wear it any other way because any other way directed eyes to me—and history told me that was never a good thing. However, being able to apply makeup to cover bruises had proved useful for all three of us over the years. On this day, I needed no such skill, just a mask of confidence, of independence, should the meeting hit the fan.

Guards brought in inmates, and I anxiously gazed at them all. Not recognising my father was another nightmare I had been having since deciding to confront him before anyone else. That fear, at least, was squashed the second he walked into the room and it would only take a second more for me to realise the next nightmare was also unfounded.

"*Cassie!*" he declared the moment our eyes locked. Our matching brown eyes.

My body longed to hug him but prison rules did not allow for it. Instead, we silently beamed at each other until our hearts stilled long enough for us to speak.

"You came." His voice crackled, but it was the same voice I remembered. "I'm so happy you came." There was no reproach, no anger, only relief.

Swallowing the knot in my throat, I replied, "I didn't know you wanted me to come."

His strong, masculine face twisted in pain. "Oh, Cassie... Oh, my girl." His nostrils flared as he struggled to find words.

"Mum redirected the mail. Until a few days ago I hadn't read a single letter you wrote." I chuckled softly. "It took me a while, but I've read them all now."

We chatted. Tears flowed. We chatted some more.

Dad tried to control his anger towards Mum, especially after I told him she was dead, but I could see it took a huge amount of effort for him not to say *good*. Had I told him all about my childhood, I doubt he would have refrained.

In a moment's pause, my heart felt heavy.

Closing my eyes, I whispered, "Please forgive me."

"What for?"

"For taking so long to get here."

"My love, you have always been here," Dad said, holding his hands across his heart.

A sob choked me as I felt the wave of his affection. I felt loved. Mimicking his action, I nodded, smiling through my tears.

Somewhere in my swirling emotions, my mission for answers, not just a connection returned. "What happened? Why did

Mum do this? Why did Gary do this? I thought he still visited you?"

"Gary does. Less than he used to, but he comes when he has business to discuss. I thought it was him today when I got the call saying I had a visitor. He failed to mention about you or your mum though. He said Michelle cut all ties with him, too."

"But why?"

Almost turning himself into a wall, Dad straightened his broad, muscled shoulders—obviously, he continued to work out in prison—and for a moment I feared he wasn't going to answer. Narrowing his eyes as though he were testing my resolve, he spoke in a low voice, "What do you remember? Around the time I went away—what do you remember?"

"Very little. The police took you away after that guy died. Gary was at home a lot but struggled to hold onto the reins of the business so Darren split it for a few years until..." Painful memories swamped me, and I ran out of words.

Dad grimaced. "Before that, honey, before I was taken. What do you remember?"

My nose wrinkled under my glasses. "What do you mean? We were happy. You had a healthy, solid business and were very busy, but we were happy—right?" Suddenly I feared that the only piece of happiness I held on to was also a lie.

"We were." Dad smiled. "We were always two peas, bound together, you and I."

"But?" There had to be a *but*...

"But your mother and I were not so solid. In truth, *she* was not always so solid. She wanted more attention, more excitement. I was busy. She—"

"Had an affair?" Disgust, not surprise, filled me.

"She did."

"And you're in for his murder?" I had always been told it was a drug deal gone bad, but now I knew otherwise.

"For the assassin's murder."

My mouth gaped. "A hitman?" Dad held his finger to his mouth, so I continued in a hushed voice. "Do you mean the lover hired a hitman?"

"More of a drug addict gambler who owed a few too many favours and had zero problems paying them off by any means, but yes."

"Who did he owe the most?" I knew the answer before it left my father's lips.

"Your uncle."

As the blood drained from my face, I hid it in my hands. Dad reached across the table and gently stroked my hair, but a guard quickly reminded him of the rules. All eyes turned to us, Dad held up his hands in submission, and slowly we were ignored again.

My mind raced. The angry mouse was back—darting inside my head, giving me a splitting headache. "Why are you here, not him?"

Dad's face softened. "That part of the past is something I do not regret. I serve my time without lament, my darling."

"But Gary runs your businesses! Why? Why, when he caused all of this?"

"Sometimes it's better the devil you know." He tilted his head. "And this devil doesn't know all I do, so he thinks he has the upper hand. In his own way, he also works for a similar goal."

"Oh?"

"Family." He scoffed. "Family and money—he always did love the power of money."

"But he has no family. No wife, no kids—*fuck, no.*" It felt weird swearing in front of my dad for the first time but the fear that I was not talking to my father cut me deeply. I had to know. "Am I not yours?"

"Always." Dad said with heart. "Never doubt it. *I am* your father."

"But?" I barely whispered.

"*But* your uncle thought you were his daughter. You *could* have been his—I think your mum led him to believe so—but unknown to them when you were a baby, I had my suspicions so I bought one of those family tree DNA kits which proved otherwise. Stupidly, I then ignored my doubts about them, but I think it is fair to say that your mother and Gary had an on-off relationship for many years. It almost cost my bloody business as his disloyalty caused such tension with the crew they split in two for a while." Dad sneered. "Thankfully others have proved more trustworthy."

"Yet, Mum didn't stay with Gary. She went with Darren. Why?"

"She went with the power. When that blew up in her face, she gave up and sought attention elsewhere, I guess."

What he said made sense but made me feel physically ill.

All memory of *elsewhere* made me sick.

"If Gary—what, out of jealousy, hired the hit on you, why is he in charge of your company? And trustee of my finances?" I was repeating myself but it still made no sense.

"Because he knows the business and is family. Despite everything, I can control him because he doesn't realise that I know all. He thinks I bought the whole *we were attacked by a disgruntled junkie-cum-burglar* lie that he cooked up. He knows that without me, even stuck in here, he has nothing. Michelle walked away from him when I left. The guys almost did, too. We work by loyalty, and I hold the pay cheques." He smiled. "And on one vital goal we agree."

"Which is?"

"You, Cassie. Family dynasty. You have always been the future. Despite everything, we love you unreservedly. Michelle might have thrown spanners in the way but all is for you. Every dime, every drop of blood. *You will rise.* I took the reins from my father, and when you are ready, you will do the same—and then, my dear, it will all have been worth it."

"But I can't pretend, Dad. I don't think I can pretend to be his loving niece knowing all this. For so long, something has been holding me back. Until now I didn't know what it was. I thought it was pain from my past—scars that made me sceptical. Now I think it was a piece of you telling me to be on my guard. A sixth sense." I desperately wanted to reach across the table. "What do you want me to do?"

"Get Gary to teach you everything."

"That will take years."

"So?" Dad shrugged. "Are you going to university?"

"Yes...yes, I've been thinking that I'd like to do both landscaping and business studies. They're very different, I know. Mum wouldn't have been keen, but—"

"Cassie, if that is what you want, I could not be prouder."

"But my rise will take—"

"As long as it takes." His smile seeped into my pores like sunshine. The warmth that I had been starved of for so long. "You are mine, Cassie. You are everything. From the moment you opened your eyes, I saw you. I saw me in you and you in me. Everything else is just noise. Absorb Gary's knowledge, establish yourself as head of the company. Your uncle's karma will wait."

REVELATION

Secrecy was essential, so I took all of Dad's letters to our old house and burnt them, leaving the ashes to dry and float around the woods as though I were mourning his loss all over again. In part I was, yet something else had been born. A hope. A purpose.

It was impossible not to watch Gary with a sense of disgust when I got home that night but I also felt dirty. Somehow I always ended up feeling dirty. I was the strange prize in a game of power, yet no one had truly claimed me because something inevitably happened to make me slip between their fingers—even when they wanted to hold on.

You rattled around me, and I tutted at myself. *Except you, You, but you have no fingers to slip through.*

Silently eating the spaghetti Bolognese Gary had made, questions mushroomed in my head, and I prayed Dad's patience would rub off on me.

"What's up?" Gary said between mouthfuls. "School bad?"

School was always bad. I would finish what I started because I had a plan for beyond those school gates—plus the summer break was just days away to give me some respite—but cold stares, sneers, and enforced solitary confinement made every day a trial. I didn't even have the quiet, but calm companionship in lessons of Nic Reid anymore because he went to college instead of doing A levels. Had Mum let me, I would have done the same. But like I said, I now had a plan and that involved making no big waves, so I would finish what I'd started.

"Or is it that Freddie kid?" Daydreaming and still chewing my food, I hadn't answered Gary's first question. He met my blank stare with a grin. "He came by earlier. He said you hadn't answered his calls…"

"Oh." Twisting pasta into control, I loaded my fork instead of maintaining eye contact. "Did he say what he wanted?"

"No. Just to talk to you—or maybe something about a picnic. I put on the overbearing parent act to test him out. Then I offered him drugs to really test him." He stopped, smirking, but his amusement burst out loud when he saw my shocked face.

"You didn't?" The more amused he looked, the angrier I felt, but I could see Gary didn't understand the full extent of my rage. Honestly, I knew he wouldn't risk anyone knowing what was downstairs, yet the thought of endangering Freddie made me queasy—but not as nauseous as the realisation that Gary was coming to believe that he had the right to play the role of my father. Instantly, I knew I had to keep Freddie away from this place. Away from me.

"Oh, relax! I'm only messing with you. Why are you so serious? Did you fight? Do I need to kill him?"

His tone made me do anything *but* relax. My mind jumped to us half naked, me screaming, holding a lump of wood. "No.

I just don't feel like talking to him. We're just friends anyway."
Or were.

Gary laughed. *"Sure, you are."*

The summer of my seventeenth year was eye opening. I promised myself the summer holidays would be a mixture of work and relaxation. The former was easy. The family business was there in all its glory and Gary proudly introduced me to his real estate team, making it very clear that my interest in landscape and design could very easily flourish there—pun intended.

There was literally a team for everything. Buying, selling, construction, renovation, demolition, maintenance, and everything in between. The Reilly Corporation was everywhere in and around town. The only reason people didn't know was because the spider legs had multiple names. The body had many eyes. But the heart was Reilly. Of course, the blood was white and powdered—but that was a detail for another name.

After long days at work, I longed to walk in the woods. No one openly sneered at me anymore, and I wore the clothes and persona befitting what Gary wanted me to be, but that again stopped me from appealing to anyone on a more personal level.

"You can't earn respect and be their best friends," Gary told me on my first day. "You have your loyal circle. That comes with time, but mostly money. Everyone else is below you. Remember that, Cassie. Only *we* are at the top."

Something kept me from disturbing the wild peace of the woods where I once called home. Visiting occasionally was alright, but my skin prickled as though I was not yet ready to go back. Maybe I should have, but when overwhelmed

I drove to the spot Mum taught me to drive and cried uninhibitedly—until the locals turned up.

Freddie had stopped calling. At first I was surprised he called, then annoyed that he wouldn't just leave me alone—then sad when he did. It was for the best but I acutely felt the loneliness of an empty voice and mailbox. Joey was busy more often than not and if I saw him I was usually asked to taxi him and his friends somewhere. I never said no though.

Joey's latest request was to escort him to a gig in the town hall where his friend's older brothers were playing in a band. Despite me practicing my supportive sister enthusiasm before we arrived, they were actually pretty good.

Fading into the background was my speciality, so I picked a stool in the corner at the bar, ordered an orange juice and packet of crisps, and silently acknowledged there were worse ways to spend my Saturday night. Bodies bumping against me as they ordered their beverages was my only real gripe, but they went as quickly as they came so even that was manageable.

"Three beers, and a coke, please," a male voice said to the barman ridiculously close to my right ear.

Automatically, I turned, and saw Nic Reid's eyes gazing into mine. In any other situation, I would have blushed and run, pretending not to have seen him, but as we were millimetres from one another, I was somewhat trapped.

"Hey," I said coyly.

"Hey, Cassie. It's good to see you." Nic ruffled his hair awkwardly. "Sorry, I didn't mean to shout my order in your ear."

"No problem." I laughed. "How are you?"

"Yeah, I'm good, thanks. You?" His eyes drifted up and down my body. "You look good."

"Can't complain." Against my better judgement, I found myself checking him out. It had been a year since I had seen him and time had been very kind to his already handsome features. Possibly it had been to me too, I wasn't sure—but Nic's expression told me there was an improvement.

"How's your sister?" I asked, wanting to change the subject.

"Ursula's well, thanks. Cheeky as ever—although she can't see white vans or sweet bags without shuddering."

"I'm not surprised." We both grimaced.

A hand appeared on his left shoulder. "Hey, Nicky, where's the drinks?" a boy jovially said. "We're waiting, you know."

"Haha, you mean, *you* are waiting! Here, take them. I'll be there in a minute." Without attempting to introduce me, Nic passed three of the drinks to his friend and sat down on the stool next to me.

"College friends?" I asked.

"Yeah." He smiled. "One's my girlfriend, actually."

Disappointment flashed through me but I laughed at myself as a new, unchecked, thought bubbled out of my mouth. "As long as it isn't Kimberley Jenkins, I'm happy for you!"

Nic almost snorted. "No, it's safe to say I'm over that stage!"

"Excellent."

"You had a shit show at school thanks to her, didn't you." That wasn't a question, only a melancholic statement of my childhood. "I wanted to be friends. You know that, right? I should have—"

"It's okay. Kimberley and I blank each other these days and I'm counting down to my freedom." *In more ways than one.* "I envy you yours, though—but thank you for being a calmer spot in her storm for all those years."

Nic nodded, then suddenly laughed heartily as though I had told him an amazing joke. "She's a nasty cow, but you gave some good ones back!"

I sniggered. "Yeah."

His face became more serious as he travelled further down memory lane. "Some of it was freaky though. When you screamed—"

He cut himself off and my memory raced to me shouting at Mr Yates, our teacher, as though he were trying to rape me. That was mortifying. The teacher was a douchebag, but he wasn't Gordon.

That bastard soils every potential connection I try to make, I said to myself. "Fuck. Yeah, that was embarrassing. My head hurt after."

"I bet."

"Don't get me wrong, Mr Yates was an idiot, but I overreacted, I—"

"What? Oh yeah, that was an *interesting* day, too." Nic ruffled his hair again. I didn't know whether that was a good thing or not. He always did it when he was nervous. Memory lane for me was a thousand times worse than for him, so it didn't feel fair that he was more notably affected.

"Wait. What day were you thinking of?" I said, although Nic hadn't moved from his stool.

Again, Nic's fingers ran through his hair. "The day Kim and her mates ambushed you after art and ruined your painting."

"Huh." I scuffed my foot on the ledge around the bar. "I was upset that day."

Raising his eyebrows, Nic softly chuckled. "I could tell!"

Despite the laughter, I sensed restraint in his tone and his eyes added a sentence that I could not quite understand. To date, I had never asked what anyone else saw when You defended me. As no one had said anything, I imagined they either saw nothing or respected and feared my friend enough to be silent. For me, events always played out as though seen in an angry haze or as if watching a scary scene in a movie from behind a cushion—I saw enough to know what happened but didn't necessarily recall or require intimate detail of You's actions. Suddenly that changed.

"What did you see?"

Nic's face fell. "What do you mean?"

"You saw Kim attack me, right?" Nic nodded. "Then what?"

"I saw you cry out in pain and anger—*rightly so*—" Nic paled. I waved my hand for him to continue. "And then you grabbed her."

"That's it?"

"Well, no. You grabbed her tongue until she screamed and bit into her tongue so hard that blood dribbled down her face."

"But what did You look like? What did you see precisely?"

Nic's beautiful face screwed up. "What do you mean, Cassie? Why are you talking about yourself in third person? You were right to be fucking mad. The more I think about Kim's actions, the more ashamed I am that I ever spoke to her, let alone dated her, but you were pretty wild that day." He put his hands up as though he were surrendering to me. "No judgement, though, okay?"

I stared at him, smiling. It was a painted smile to hide the chaos within, but it was enough to make his shoulders relax and encourage his wide smile to return. It felt like Nic had clicked a lightbulb on in the darkness, and now I knew where the switch was.

Finally.

Having dropped Joey off at the pony club summer camp, I sat in the car, smiling to myself. Joey looked so cute in his jodhpurs, shirt, and riding hat as he and his friends gathered around the arena with their ponies. Through the window, I took a photo and realised I wanted to send it to Freddie. Possibly Joey would show him pictures anyway, they still texted each other, but I wanted to share the moment with Freddie myself.

As much as I told myself I didn't miss him, I did. Wasn't I being more honest, more in control of myself these days? Couldn't that involve talking to Freddie? He was a friend, especially after Mum died. He was there when I found the PO Box letter—although it was probably a blessing he didn't see me read Dad's letters...or know that I had seen my father. Secrets were always easier to keep alone.

Starting the engine, I backed out of the parking space, leaving Joey in my rearview mirror and paused at the end of the drive, waiting for traffic to pass. Tapping the break propelled a small, green lunch box from under the passenger seat, causing me to groan. Putting the car into reverse, I returned to the yard, bent over to grab the box and my fingers brushed the side of another.

"For fucks sake, Joey," I muttered to myself. "How much crap have you left in my—"

I didn't finish my sentence. The second box wasn't Joey's.

It seemed impossible that I had forgotten about the parcel in Mum's PO Box, yet in my hurry to read the letters, I had placed it under the passenger seat in my car and become so absorbed in the messages that all else had faded away.

Before memories blurred again, I ran to Joey, delivered his lunch box, and returned to the car. You whispered to drive away, and I reluctantly agreed. Whether by subconscious choice, deliberate design, or destiny I do not truly know, but I parked the car in a layby on the edge of the woods that ran behind Fred Forde's holiday lets.

Staring at the cardboard box, my brain started to play *guess the contents.*

It made my temples pulsate.

Get a grip, I told myself. *It's been in your car for weeks. Just open it!*

Running my key through the seal, I popped open the box, making sure I didn't disturb Mum's beautiful handwritten label. It's funny what becomes a treasure when it cannot be replaced. As it turned out, the parcel contained two irreplaceable things: Mum's writing and the penknife Dad gave me as a child.

A note simply read: *We must protect that which cannot be lost.*

Trying not to spill the foam packaging balls, I searched the box but nothing else was there. No explanation, no clues, no reason, yet it was enough to spark tears. That knife was the symbol of my father's trust in me as an apprentice gardener, but it disappeared around the time I lost him.

Now both were found.

A shadow cast over the driver's side of the car, and I squealed.

"Shit, sorry!" Freddie called through the closed window, stepping away.

"Hey, Freddie." I hurriedly opened the door, trying not to appear flustered.

"I didn't mean to frighten you. I just drove home and saw your car, so I-I—" He rubbed the back of his neck. "Maybe I shouldn't have. Sorry."

"I didn't see you coming, that's all." I smiled as widely as I could. "I'm glad you found me."

"Yeah?" There was the cheeky grin I missed so much. "Good. Are you coming or going?" He pointed towards the woods.

"Err, coming. I haven't seen my garden for...well, since I saw you last. I thought I'd have a little wander." *Just break the damn ice and say, since I fucked up and screamed at you.* Why was talking when it mattered so bloody hard?

Freddie scuffed his foot in the dry grass. "I miss you, Cassie."

My heart pounded in my chest. "I miss you, too."

I didn't think his cheeky grin could get any wider. I was wrong. Even when nervous, his smile could melt a thousand hearts. "I'm sorry," he said, suddenly dropping the grin. "About before, I wanted to... I—"

Closing the gap between us, I gently grabbed both his cheeks and kissed him. It took all of a few seconds for him to wrap his arms around me and it felt amazing. Safe. The difference between then and now wasn't Freddie though. It was me. Slowly, I was beginning to understand myself. To trust myself.

"I'm the one who is sorry," I said, linking my arms behind his neck. "There is a part of me, a history. It marks me. You're better off without it, but I wanted to say sorry, to—"

Apparently, we were equally good at stopping each other from saying stupid things, and it was Freddie's turn to cut me off with a kiss. Stepping back, I took him by the hand and led him into the woods.

When we reached my wild garden, I expected to find it withered and dead thanks to the recent heat, yet it bloomed beautifully. Although not one for dancing, I came pretty close as I wandered around the flowers. "You watered it?" Freddie nodded. "You carted water out here—why?"

"I'd have thought that was obvious." He coyly sniggered. "For you."

My heart swelled so much, I almost ran at him. He met me in the middle and kissed me. At first it was heated but gentle, then every touch grew stronger, deeper, more needy. Freddie pulled back. His eyes searched mine for direction. Should he go further? Should he stop? He waited for me. Equally afraid to break the spell as I was of being visited by past ghosts, I chewed on my lip.

You sent electricity down my back. *You are in control*, they said.

Closing the gap again, I pulled Freddie's t-shirt over his head, my lips tasting every inch from his neck to his navel. He shuddered with each move. Gently, so gently, he ran his hands around the bottom of my vest. Raising my arms, I let him undress me, taking his time to slip my bra straps off my shoulders, and unhook the back. He caressed my stomach and chest with his lips, then worked up to my throat and mouth. Our bodies were awash with sweat, and I could feel that he was yearning to take me as much as I was yearning to be taken. He didn't dare though. Memory served him well. We had been this far before.

I shivered.

You are in control, You repeated.

Exhaling deeply, I unzipped his jeans and reduced him to his pants, then took those too. He continued to wrap me in his arms, kissing me but wouldn't touch my trousers. If I wanted this, I had to do it. Slipping my hand inside the elasticated rim, I pulled my trousers down and kicked them off in one motion along with my knickers.

Freddie gulped. Our hearts raced.

Sit down, I whispered, nibbling on his earlobe.

Without question, he sat on the dry, woodland floor, and stretched his arms out to me. Carefully lowering myself onto him, I let out a chastened gasp as our bodies linked. In slow, gentle, unity, we found the sweet joy of ecstasy.

Despite being accompanied by pleasant thoughts of Freddie, the drive to prison seemed longer the next time I visited. The weather was good and nothing bad had happened, but I was determined to ask my father the questions that plagued me.

"Dad, I need you to tell me the truth."

"Always, honey, always," Dad replied as he sat with his hands resting on the cold beige table across from me.

Sitting up straight, I cleared my throat. "The hitman. Did you really shoot him?"

Dad chewed on his bottom lip. He could see where this conversation was going. "I did."

"Truthfully?"

"Truthfully."

"Where?"

"In the back. Three times."

"No, where was he?"

"Running down the fucking street—well, trying to."

"And why was he trying to run down the street?"

"Because I was coming after him with a gun, honey. People tend to run when you do that."

"You said he was *trying to run*. Was he not running very well?"

Dad grunted. "No, he wasn't. I guess you'd call it somewhere between a shuffle and a crawl by the time he stopped."

"And why was that?"

"Because he was cut to shit and bleeding."

"So the bullets just finished him off?"

"So the bullets just finished him off, yes, Cassie."

"If he hadn't been in the street, you wouldn't have been caught, would you?" Tears now rose in my eyes.

Dad didn't answer for a moment. I flexed and rolled my wrist towards him.

He shook his head.

"And whose fault is that?" I asked, gulping hard.

"Cassie, honey, there is no point going over this." Dad put his hands together in a praying motion. "It is what it is."

"Answer the question. You promised to tell me the truth. Whose fault is it the hitman got on the street for all the fucking neighbours to see in his bloodied state?"

Dad's eyes glanced everywhere except at me. Eventually, he turned to me and a tear rolled down his cheek. "Yours."

If a world-class boxer had punched me in the stomach, I doubt it would have hurt or winded me less than the force that hit me in that moment. The dreams were memory. The nightmares were memory. And now I knew.

Uninterested in the action movie, that night Mum had gone upstairs to bed and left Dad and me curled up on the sofa. With the exception of a lamp on the coffee table on the other side of the room, the lights were out and midway through the film I fell asleep. With speakers everywhere, Dad loved his sound system and while fictional cars blew up, unknown to us a man crept through the backdoor into the kitchen. Waking up in time to see the end credits of the film, I was thirsty. Sliding off the sofa, I wandered across the living room with bleary vision in the direction of the kitchen just as it swung open, causing me to let out an almighty squeal. The intruder paused. I wasn't part of his plan. Wasting no time, Dad sprung to his feet, charging in our direction. The man clumsily aimed his gun and fired. Dad dodged, narrowly avoiding the straying bullet before launching himself at our attacker.

Never being one to shy away from standing with my beloved father, I reached into my pocket and retrieved my prized seventh birthday present—the silver folding knife. The men wrestled, punching and kicking, each trying to turn the gun on the other. Throwing myself at the hitman, I slashed at his wrist and the gun tumbled to the floor. Dad kicked it away, the man spat, thumped me, then dropped his shoulder and flew into Dad's chest with all his might.

Grabbing the lamp, the hitman smashed it over Dad's head, causing him to slump to the floor, and hit his head on the edge of the table on the way down, knocking him unconscious. Smirking, the hitman's eyes darted around him, looking for his gun so he could finish his task. Fury blazed through me as I threw myself, blade first, at his ankles and hastily worked my frenzied hand up as high as I could given my size.

In a desperate bid to stop me slashing him, he pushed me backwards, desperately searching for his weapon. Thrusting my hand back in a bid to get up, my fingers curled around the smooth barrel of the gun. Hearing it move on the cold, stone floor, the hitman turned to me just as I pointed it at him.

He ran.

I fired—and missed.

Not ready to give up, I ran down the drive after him with my mother's screams echoing behind me as she came downstairs and found my father.

The hitman made it to the street before he paused, heaving from pain and exhaustion. Hearing my footsteps, he turned. For a split second I could see him deciding whether to challenge me or try to run again.

I didn't pause.

Aiming the gun, I shot.

I missed.

He ran.

I shot again and he dropped to the ground just as Dad, holding his side, breathing heavily, ran up next to me. Wordlessly, his hand gently moved down my arm until it reached the gun which still pointed at the groaning figure crawling on the rain-soaked road.

Seeing my father alive, my anger tempered. He smiled at me with tears in his eyes—tears of pride and love—until Mum ran up beside us and his face switched into action.

"Get her indoors." He said with cold, calm authority. "Different clothes. Hide the knife. Go straight to bed—both of you."

Sobbing, Mum swooped me up and ran.

When the front door had less than an inch left to close, the sound of neighbours screaming and three bullets firing broke the silence of the night. Trembling, Mum did exactly as my father directed, but neither of us slept. Although I cannot ask her, I'm guessing in the days that followed, she opened a PO Box and mailed herself a parcel. What I do know is before long, we were called outside again by blue lights and screaming sirens—and my father was taken away.

My body felt limp. Had I aimed higher, deeper, or just kept out of the way, Dad could have bested the hitman faster. He would never have left the house if Dad were not defending me. Kimberley Jenkins was right. I was a Jailbird. Only the wrong person was caged.

"I'm so sorry," I whispered through tear-choked breaths. "It should be me in here—"

"Never think that."

"But I—"

"*Saved me.*" Dad smiled.

"You don't know that. If I weren't there, if I had kept out the way, you wouldn't have—"

"Cassie, my darling, if you were not there, nothing else would have mattered."

THE WINNER TAKES ALL

The game of life is a curious one. We are all born into it without a say where we land on the board. Sometimes we roll the dice and it unreservedly falls in our favour, other times we have to crawl along, step by painful step, hoping the players around us don't crush us on their route to the finish line. Then there are the wildcards, the spins of the wheel, who lift, who offer a hand when you stumble—the good eggs who make life better. And finally, there are those who make their own rules. Who bleed, sweat, and cry their way to the top—or to each other. Who bide their time. Dad and I are two such players. Fortune favours the brave, but also the underhand—as proved by my uncle. Yet even he acted out of love. Misplaced love; but love all the same.

"Gary?" I said, sitting at the breakfast bar the morning of my twenty-first birthday.

"Yes, Cassie?"

"Do you remember, a long time ago, asking me what I wanted to do with the site of my old house?"

"I do," he smiled amusedly, just like he did when I was little and wanted sweets.

"Well, I'd like to build a new house." Gary stared at me. "Not like the old one though. I want us to leave this place to employees. Distance ourselves from work, you know? Something different where we can start anew—*together*."

Dad was right, the idea of a united family did light Gary up. He hated it when I was away at university, so when I came home he couldn't hide his pleasure—nor leave me to any peace in my annex. Despite everything in the past, I loved him for it. Gary never confessed to hiring someone to try and kill my father, and I never asked. I knew the truth, and that was enough. It was as though my brain settled once I had answers. The only thing I did not understand was why Gary kept away for so much of my childhood. It made no sense to me.

"I'd love that," Gary replied with heart. "It will take a while, but—"

"I will be home permanently from next summer and going fulltime in the company. I was hoping it could be ready then. Is that doable?"

"Absolutely."

"Fantastic. I've been secretly making plans..." I reached into my bag and pulled out my sketches. Sketches that Dad and I had been working on, but I made sure there was no hint of his input for Gary to detect.

Flattening the paper on the counter, I watched Gary's face beam. "Perfect."

"I want it to be different from the old place. You know, only save the good memories?" Keeping my eyes on my uncle, I waited to see if he would drop into the line of conversation I was hoping for. "*No workers*." My repetition was no accident.

"Yeah, definitely," he said thoughtfully. "Your mum would be rejoicing if she heard that."

Bingo. "Oh? Did she tell you not to live where you work?" I said, innocently.

Gary scoffed. "Numerous times. I built this place for her—plus you and Joey—but she refused to come here unless she was absolutely destitute." His face and tone darkened. "Ha! Even then she chose a fucking campervan and holiday park cleaning toilets over me."

"Why did you not insist? If you loved her so much?" I was on dangerous ground. Gary had never confessed his love, but I needed that last jigsaw piece. Admitting I understood the bigger picture was the only way to get it.

Relief wasn't what I expected to see in Gary's eyes, but that is exactly the feeling he displayed—like I had just relieved him of an almighty burden. "She's the only woman I've ever loved—besides you, and that's different."

"But you were never properly together?"

"Officially, no. She married your dad knowing I loved her. She loved us both, I am sure of it, but she went with the leader. She always did. She shone with whoever served her better." Gary shook his head. "After Darren died she had enough of being *the boss's wife.* She didn't want to be around the crew or our merchandise, and I was building an empire...expanding the family empire—"

"*Under your house.*"

"I thought she'd come round, you know, like she always did. I wanted to adopt you. Did she tell you?" I shook my head. He sneered. "Figures because instead she threatened to report the whole fucking business to the cops if I came anywhere near you again. She knew I'd never hurt either of you, so I did what she asked and kept my love for her a secret—but she burnt me anyway."

We stared at each other through blurred vision.

"She was forever chasing the idea of family or fortune somewhere," Gary whispered.
Pot. Kettle. Black.
Those three words ran through my mind.
Inside I screamed while You buzzed.
We knew what colour we were.

After delivering the plans to Gary, I promised not to visit my old house until the work was done. Having waited so long for a place to truly call home, a few more months should not have been an issue, but they dragged. Graduation came and went, I took my place in the firm—there was still much to learn, but all those who needed to know me, did. Everything else ticked over like a well-oiled machine.

My list of friends was still shorter than one hand. I was still the weird girl, but I was the weird girl with power, with associates—and a mean looking baseball bat. I still called it Gordon's, even after it had had an upgrade. One day, when Freddie and I were walking hand-in-hand, we found a broken strand of barbed wire on the side of a cattle field. Having travelled to the beach and hiked into the nearby countryside, it was supposed to be a romantic day out of town, so Freddie questioned why I would want it, but I carried it back to the car and he chose not to ask again. He was wise like that. After telling him plainly we would break up forever if he visited my home, he knew enough to agree to stay away from my uncle. Gary's jealous taunts had too much weight, so I decided a broken heart but alive would be better than dead or severely injured.

When the longed-for day arrived, I buzzed with anticipation. So much so, I feared that I would ruin it all. The timing had to be perfect, which was difficult when not everything was under my control, but after sweet talking some of the builders, I knew when the house was done and managed to delay until all the stars aligned.

Everything was furnished and decorated. All I had to do was pack my bags and walk through the front door. Once upon a time, that packing would require less than one suitcase, now I had acquired many more. Gazing in the mirror, I could not see Cassie Reilly aged seven, or ten. The awkward girl in baggy clothes, messy hair, and ill-suited glasses. Now I looked tamed. I looked purposeful, but You knew what raged inside. The girl who had avoided, dreaded violence, had found it all the same. It shaped her, but it would not define. I would choose.

"It's beautiful," I gushed, walking through the front door of the log cabin-style house for the first time. "It's even better than I imagined!" Turning around, I saw the emotion in Gary's eyes. "Thank you," I said, kissing his cheek.

"My pleasure, but I just realised your vision, honey. Today is a new start."

Smiling broadly, I met his gaze. "Absolutely."

Walking through the house, I was relieved to find it wholly different to the house I had grown up in. There would be no daily reminders within these walls. Only the outside held ghosts, but there, at the bottom of the garden, I wanted to hold onto the past and mix it with the future. Just as nature had turned everything into a wilderness, I wanted my little patch to evolve too.

"Can we see the garden?" I asked, grabbing my uncle by the hand.

Laughing, Gary didn't resist. A pristine lawn had been reclaimed and a vegetable patch cultivated ready for me to plant, but everything else was wild, just as I requested.

The redbrick shed with flint remained largely covered, but the wooden door had been liberated and painted and someone had placed a horseshoe in the centre of the frame with the tips pointing upwards. *To catch the devil,* I thought to myself.

We did not go inside the shed. It was not yet my time.

"I spent hours in these woods," I said, staring up at the enormous trunks in awe.

"I know, you loved it out here." Gary leaned against an ash tree. "If ever we couldn't find you, you were always here—or in that shed."

"Dad taught me so much about plants out here," I said, knowing I was breaking our one unspoken rule. Gary grimaced, but I wasn't done. Today was the day for change. "You remember, right?"

"Of course."

"Your dad, my grandad, loved growing things too, right? That's how this whole dynasty started?"

"It was comparatively small potatoes back then, but yes, you know that's true." Gary held my arm, peering into my eyes. "What is it, Cassie? What aren't you saying?"

"Family is everything. The future." A tear rolled down my cheek.

"*Everything,*" Gary repeated, brushing my face with the palm of his hand.

"Then why did you try to kill your brother?"

Gary's face turned to stone. Very pale, sickly stone.

"And why did you then tell me for years that my father wanted nothing to do with me—like his incarceration was my fault, *not yours*. I didn't send a fucking hitman after him so you could try to steal his business, wife, and daughter." My tone dropped but remained steady. I had waited fourteen years to make this speech. I wasn't going to blub through it now.

Gary, however, was.

"Who told you?" he whimpered. In an instant, the cocky, self-assured gangster had crumbled. He had only one Achilles heel and it was finally biting back.

"So you don't deny it?"

Gary sighed. "What's the point? All I've done is love you, Cassie. You are mine, in my heart. For a while I thought you were actually mine, your mum said you were, but it doesn't matter. You are my family. The future. Your dad said that, too. He understands that much."

I raised an eyebrow. "That much?"

"He and your mother thought it was a burglar who attacked the house."

"Mum might have," I snapped, "but Dad does not."

Gary tilted his head. "*Does not?* You've seen him? When?"

Ignoring his question, I asked the only one that I still needed answered, even if I already thought I knew the truth. "Why did you and Mum hide me from him?"

"To move on." Gary swore under his breath. "We all needed to move on. This changes nothing, Cassie. Why bring it up now? I am sorry, for what it is worth. Jacob and I—your dad and I—we had our moments, but I have diligently guided the business as he asked since then. Jealousy ate at me. I was younger, stupider back then. If he can forgive, I hope you can, too."

A deep voice cleared behind my uncle as a figure stepped out of the shed. "I do *not* forgive you."

Gary spun around and stared his brother in the eyes. "*Jacob?*" He glanced back and forth between my father and me. "What the fuck? You're free? Your sentence isn't done yet?"

"Good behaviour, little brother, good behaviour." My father spread his arms as if embracing nature. "It is rewarded!"

"As is patience," I said, reaching around a tree and curling my fingers around the handle of Gordon's bat. I didn't wait for a response. The time for talking was over. Only swinging.

The barbed wire I stapled into the bat proved effective. It was a shame I hadn't thought of that when justice revisited Hal and Gordon a few weeks earlier. For them, I only heard about the end results, and although effective, both events were less dramatic. For Gordon it was a simple car accident leaving the dogging site. Two of my guys giggled as they told me where they had followed him to. The realisation that my mother had taught me to drive where she and her perverted ex-boyfriend had done it just cemented my request.

This time was different.

More personal.

We had to serve justice—or revenge.

"Do you need a hand, honey?" my father asked.

Pausing, we smiled at him. "No Daddy, not this time. We've got this."

*At the bottom of the garden lived many creatures
all of which I now knew
And there, I bonded with an elusive soul
simply referred to as 'You'*

*In my childish memory, I had blanked out so much
it was a shame
For I didn't understand my friendship
with the one with no specific name*

*They found me when I was seven
not the previously declared ten
And saved me from numerous horrors
that still plague me now and then*

*Ours was no chance encounter
it was destined in the stars
For though mother was the salt of the earth
my father is the sun, the light to heal all scars*

*And You is my keeper
and I am theirs
A friendship, a bond, a partnership
in our heart there is no room to spare*

Our uncle betrayed us
so there was only one thing to do
To learn, to wait, to bide our time,
then introduce him to You

And now he lays at the bottom of the garden
deep beneath the earth
Where only worms and beetles visit
without disturbing fresh laid turf

I take my place as Kingpin
and You and I will reign
We need no separate label
for we are one of the same

If you liked this book, please consider leaving a review on Amazon, Goodreads, or any other social media that you use. Honest reviews are invaluable to any author, but especially independent ones like Alexia.

If you would like to join Alexia's newsletter and be the first to receive updates on forthcoming novels as well as read exclusive short stories, please visit: www.alexiamuellerushbrook.co.uk

ACKNOWLEDGEMENTS

For me, writing a book can be a solitary task as the voices in my head speak out and tell their story, however, I can only finish a book with some very special helpers. Sergio, my husband, keeps me on track on the days where I flounder, tells me I can when I say I cannot, and is always first to read a manuscript, no matter how rough. He also brainstorms random details and discusses characters as though they are real—of course, to me they are, but having someone else adopt them in the early stages really drives me until I can finally write 'the end.'

But it isn't just Sergio that I have to thank. I am incredibly lucky to have found people who believe, not only in my stories, but also in me as a writer. When I asked five of them to beta read *You*, a story that is in many ways quite different to my previous works, they unreservedly agreed, and I whole-heartedly dedicate this book to them. Emma, David, Charlotte, Iona, and Kerry, you are all amazing and your friendship, feedback, and support means the world.

I cannot forget Jessica Netzke and Belle Manuel, my editors across the pond. Their support, regardless of which genre my brain has taken me into this time, is always fantastic.

To anyone who reads my work: THANK YOU! Whether you already knew me, found me through word of mouth, or discovered me via social media, the fact you took a chance on a shy, independent author is appreciated beyond words—even for a writer! When I joined the Booktok community in particular, I feared that I would simply be shouting into a void. Sometimes I still feel that way, but ultimately, I have found kindred spirits who also love stories, and to you, whether you realise it or not, I am so grateful because those connections, both from writers and readers alike, help push me on.

Here's to the next book!

ABOUT THE AUTHOR

Alexia Muelle-Rushbrook is a multi-genre author who has spent her life daydreaming in the English countryside whilst surrounded by her animals. A self-confessed geek, she has a passion for the natural world—thankfully a joy which her husband shares, otherwise the number of pets she has would drive him crazy! Stories have always run through Alexia's head, but it wasn't until one voice really wouldn't leave her alone that she realised her dream of being a writer. That voice turned into dystopian trilogy, *The Minority Rule*, but now unleashed the voices refuse to be boxed in—or limited to one genre—meaning Alexia can still be found daydreaming with her dogs but the narrative now gets recorded!

Utopia
surrounded by
dystopia,

the balance of
self, nature,
machine, secrets,
and society

has never been
so delicate

THE MINORITY RULE TRILOGY
by Alexia Muelle-Rushbrook
IS AVAILABLE TO READ NOW

When a woman is murdered by her
husband, the seaside town of Adtoft
unwittingly gains an angel.

Invisible to all, she becomes a serial
observer without hope or purpose—until
a boy falls from the Ferris wheel and
changes everything...

Alexia's paranormal mystery is available
NOW in ebook, paperback, hardcover,
and audiobook